Alice DeBerry Kane holds a BA degree from UC Santa Barbara's College of Creative Studies and an MFA from Bennington College, Vermont. A lifelong reader, writer and teacher of same, she continues to write because she enjoys the connection with readers, if only imagined. As for a writer's dream life, Alice learned early on that book tours, readings, probing questions and late nights, conflicted with her desire for solitude. And as for boxes of yellowed manuscripts stacked in storage, she quotes novelist Sylvia Plath: "Nothing stinks like a pile of unpublished writing."

Mark — I so enjoyed our visits! July 18, 2023

To K-Poo, forever in my heart – see you on the other side.

Alice DeBerry Kane

DIARY OF A DRINK

AUSTIN MACAULEY PUBLISHERS™

LONDON • CAMBRIDGE • NEW YORK • SHARJAH

A CIP catalogue record for this title is available from the British Library.

ISBN 9781528989770 (Paperback)
ISBN 9781528989787 (ePub e-book)

www.austinmacauley.com

First Published (2021)
Austin Macauley Publishers Ltd
25 Canada Square
Canary Wharf
London
E14 5LQ

"Tell me about despair, yours, and I will tell you mine."

Mary Oliver, *Wild Geese*

February 1

Hello. My name is Clare. I am not an alcoholic.

It's just after 10 a.m. and at the right of my desktop computer screen sits an eight-ounce glass of pinot noir.

Yes, pinot noir wine. I poured what was left from the open bottle I keep under the kitchen sink into a measuring cup to know for sure about the eight ounces. Before the pour, I would've guessed six, but anyone worth their wine will undersize their pour rather than be sure.

Today, I wanted to be sure. I'll finish this pour, nurse it through mid-afternoon, as I want to savour every sip, tilt the glass to note the legs, hold it up to the light to observe the ruby-rich colour, position my nose over the rim to catch the fruity aroma, still fresh, despite having been open three days. Three days – about the time it takes me to go through a bottle, by myself, because I mostly drink alone – three days from corkage to the recycle bin.

I chose February to throw down this gauntlet because it's the shortest month of the year. In the old days when I was a practising Catholic, I would have chosen the first day of Lent to declare a forty-day abstinence: give up bread, give up bingo, give up booze. No, forty days of Lent is too long. I will set upon beginning my resolve today, this first of twenty-eight days, because it's a short month and because I'm ready.

Besides, there's a loophole in my Catholic Lent that Sundays don't really count. No give-ups demanded on Sundays in Lent. God wants us to rest, even from self-imposed sacrifice. Knowing me (and who would better), when a Sunday rolled around, I would excuse myself in Lent because Sundays don't count; I would cheat and reach for the drink calling out to me from under the sink.

So, I've settled on today, February 1, to resolve to abstain from alcohol, specifically wine, for an entire month. Yes, I know, this should mean I start today. But I can't waste this last half pint of pinot noir already poured, patiently awaiting me from the right of my screen, can't put the genie back into the bottle. Can I? Would you? So, let's rephrase: I'll resolve today and act tomorrow.

Why? you ask. What am I trying to prove? That I am not an alcoholic. I can count on one hand the times I've been drunk. I can't stand myself drunk. I can't stand a headache or having to hover over a toilet bowl while I discharge the slimy chunky off-colour contents of my gut after a drunk; I can't stand the retching, the stench, the point of no return that leads to regret and a swear to quit. I don't respect myself drunk.

My goal: to abstain from everything alcohol for one month, as soon as I finish this drink.

February 2

Unseasonably warm. But if you believe in climate change, as I do, then this unseasonably warm weather is not unusual. It's a new normal. Aside from the calamitous wind that blows through these parts, the weather is pleasant enough for me to work outside, get a jump on the real spring yet to come.

I like yard work. It's my self-prescribed drug of choice to stave off the forebodings of growing old, of succumbing to weak bones and bad cholesterol, high blood pressure, flabby heart muscle and diabetes. Oh! and skin tags, age spots, tough toenails and the urge to pee.

A friend who shares my same birthdate had her eyelids lifted – the better to see, she said – from photos she sends, I can't tell the difference, but I can't see!

I've given up yoga since moving here. While yoga is touted as the be-all remedy for what ails and for the youthfulness and vitality promised, and while I have a history for participation in the practise, I don't downward dog and plank anymore. Somehow, somewhere along the way, I acquired glaucoma. And in dealing with the consequences thereof, I've been advised to back off, as certain positions could cause more optical nerve damage and compromise my vision even further than it already has.

In its place, I practise yard work, house work and walking the dog. These are the routine activities I lean on to stay lean.

Ah, the curse of an acquired, old person's disease: glaucoma. My only safe place these days is within the brown-stuccoed walls of this tiny house, within the wire prison-fence boundary that surrounds, meant to keep the coyotes out, but dually serving to keep me in.

With old age comes fear, not only for the oncoming car I can't see off to the right or left, but also for what lurks ahead and behind. Of all the dangers that leap out as I round the corner of this last lap of life, losing eyesight has been the damn sorriest for me. Losing eyesight, losing courage, losing. I'm losing my will to fight, but not yet my will to live, if only in a semi-vegetative state. So, I'll tick off that which I can no longer do or enjoy and sit back with a glass of wine. Oh, wait, I've got twenty-eight days to go.

Yes! I say yes to yard work. That which I can still do. Rake and shovel and hoe and heave. Only the toting and heave-hoeing may also be off limits for glaucoma, but if true, I don't want to know about it, because I take pleasure in the strength in my old-lady skinniness, firm calves and butt cheeks, upper arms and abs. I feel alive when I heft and carry: bins of waste, bags of bark and mushroom compost, weighted potted patio plants. I feel a magical power when I can hoist and balance a two-cubic sack of soil amendment over a shoulder, shuffle it from the corral to the garden, split it open to spill out onto the newly hand-tilled ground. I feel a magical power when I pour a drink.

No irrigation sprinklers here and with little help from God in the form of rain or snow, I divide a five-gallon bucket of water into two metal milk pails, one for each hand, to ease the strain of schlepping water to douse the dry and fragile landscape sparsely spread over this land. This means more frequent trips but more exercise back and forth from the spigot on the patio, more chances of blindly plunging a booted foot through a gopher hole, more opportunities for cholla and cactus and wolfberry bush thorns to scrape shins, for pea-size native weed stickers to cling to socks. Highly prized piñon trees, three native nursery-bought flowering shrubs have already died due to these arid conditions, but that's the price for living in a desert where availability for water and the cost for using it are at such a premium.

Yesterday I opened an email only to learn a friend in Oregon has stage zero breast cancer. She's already gone through throat cancer and now this. A subsequent email reports that surgery revealed further spreading. She's a single, never-been-married former career woman, no children, a thousand miles away from me in a mountain cabin she retreated to after retirement. I feel helpless for her, also scared for myself. Another curse of getting older: fearing we'll (we, a collective *we*, meaning all us aging boomers who can identify with what I'm sharing) get what somebody else has got, whether disease, disaster, disability or plain bad luck. So far, I've dodged the cancer diagnosis – but not the fear – drawing a card for glaucoma instead.

While I try to read something challenging every day to stimulate my brain, the glaucoma prevents long periods of steady page turning. I ploddingly push an index finger under a sentence, pencil-circle words I do not know, or whose meanings I fail to remember – *tawdriness, solipsistic, fecund, sycophant, concupiscence* – to look up later, although my experience of late has been that even after looking up a word and with only the dog to practise my new vocabulary on, I soon forget that we, me and this word, had ever crossed paths in the first place.

Currently, I'm reading David Brook's *The Road to Character*. Actually, it's not so bad to read slowly and carefully, as I believe I digest more. I read better in the morning, when my eyes are strongest and my brain freshest. Plus, I can percolate on what I've read throughout the rest of the day. Plus, I can look up those words I do not know. The activity of looking up words in a dictionary at least makes me feel smart, if only momentarily.

Brooks, whom I've long admired as an author, critic and decent human being, gives me lots to think about. He structures his *Character* book around the stories of historical figures like St. Augustine and Dorothy Day. He writes about how they and others develop character through hardship and perseverance, how they master self-control and discipline. They also seem driven by an innate sense for their life purpose.

I struggle with that thing called life purpose, to say nothing for self-control and discipline. But to be fair, having been raised in a strict Catholic environment and having been educated in rigorously rule-based parochial schools, I do believe that early religious training has served me well. Delayed gratification comes stubbornly enough; one can't get through required Lenten fasting and required daily attendance at Holy Mass without learning that heaven with all its promises for redemption and a glorified hereafter can and does, wait. And so will the drink.

But woe is me; I'm no Dorothy Day. I cannot wait. Not another hour, not another day, to put off a drink.

February 3

Our supreme purpose in life is not to make a fortune, nor to pursue pleasure, nor to write our name on history, but to discover this spark of the divine that is in our hearts.

Eknath Easwaran

I don't know who Eknath Easwaran is, but Richard Rohr does. I'm reading Rohr simultaneous to reading Brooks. While David Brooks feeds my brain, Richard Rohr feeds my soul. I keep a copy of his inspirational booklet, *Just This,* on a shelf in my bathroom, handy for toilet and tub meditation.

This morning I read about prayer, about how prayer soothes the psyche of the one praying, much like how chanting and slipping rope or rosary beads between fingers offers a mantra, a collective *Om.* I like prayer. I pray every day. I was brought up on prayer, developed an early habit formed by teaching nuns and the Catholic Church's institutional demand for and reliance on daily prayer. When I walk my dog (rather, when she walks me) on these clay-dirt roads that whimsically snake around this squatty adobe-housed 1970s development, anyone peeking up and over their stucco-walled courtyard should not be surprised at seeing me make the sign of the cross. I sign and pray aloud, count off my blessings as a soldier counts off his steps, greet blue birds and black ravens, the occasional high-soaring hawk. I march along to my dog's cadence and my own rhythm of prayer.

The practice of daily prayer grounds me. When I pray, I connect to mysteries above and below and everything in between. Having lived at the ocean, in forests, mountains and deserts, I've learned, sometimes with mule-legged resistance, to abide in prayer; I had to learn, otherwise I would have been spirit dead a long time ago. An autopsy performed on a spirit-less corpse could list the cause of death as weakness in constitution, from complications due to and accrued from grief, loneliness, longsuffering; from the undiagnosed schizophrenic gene I carry that was my father's, Frank's. I've learned to rely on prayer to keep me sane, to keep me alive, to keep me in line. Daily prayer fastens me like Velcro to my assigned seat on the continuously rolling conveyer belt of evolving humanity and time. Rolling, rolling, rolling.

These days, at almost seventy, if I've learned anything, it's how to give up, give in, gracefully stay affixed to that seat. Prayer makes me one with God and with others, especially, with those who suffer, from disappointment, discouragement, displacement, disorientation, disenfranchisement, disease, dispiritedness, disability, distance, disparity, discrimination, disfigurement, any and all things dis—.

On the first day of my February resolution, despite the deal I made with myself over the last of that bottle of pinot noir – the eight ounces I poured into the Pyrex measuring cup which was to be my sign-off drink for the rest of the month, for the next twenty-seven days – well, despite my best intentions for testing my resolve and for discovering evidence-based benefits to health, I fell off the wagon. Plunged downward headfirst. No, not into the glass, not onto the table, certainly not over a toilet. As I said, I don't respect myself drunk. I could've confessed this fall from grace yesterday, the day after the first day, that I fell off the wagon, but I felt disinclined to admit failure.

Yes, I could pray my way through this twenty-eight-day ordeal and believe me, I've tried; this isn't my first rodeo at trying to bust this bronc. I could beg God to intervene, to forgive me each time I slip and beg I do. I admit my powerlessness over the drink. But I'm just not ready to quit entirely, because I like it too much. So, I do my best to temper this sin, stake my faith that God will forgive me in the end. (That's what Catholics do: sin and repent, then sin again and expect forgiveness again. Repeat as necessary.)

I reason, which I should never attempt, that mine is not such a grievous offense; besides, I'm not altogether convinced that I sin. I'm not altogether convinced that mine is not a pre-scripted path for me, sin and all. Come to think of it, I'm not altogether. I'm not convinced anymore what constitutes sin. Neither do I believe in hell being a destination for those who not-so grievously sin because, having lived this long through hardship, trial, unwitting and unintended offensive behaviour, having gotten this far, surely, hell is right here where I am. Surely.

Despite that by early afternoon on the first day of this self-imposed resolution, I had drained that goblet of elixir I poured from the Pyrex, when I vowed to make it my last, I found myself wanting for more. Is that what sin is, desire? Wanting for more?

17

Still, steadfastly determined to keep my vow and after spending time in the yard and time on a jigsaw puzzle begun the same day as this diary, as a way to shift my thoughts; and time on the couch sewing up the side seams to the knitted hat I had just finished and time out-the-door to brace the wind and take my dog for yet another walk – round about four p.m. – my thoughts nevertheless drifted to pouring an-end-of-day drink.

I was faced with my happy-hour habit, when I begin to roll up my sidewalks (as if I had any), when I bring in the cat and lock the doors to everything outside, when I settle in at the end of the day, when I turn to television news, *Jeopardy*! knitting, waiting. Waiting for my husband to come home from work, but in the meanwhile, I do not wait without the companionship of a drink. There I sat, on my sagging chenille-covered, arm-rest worn, cat-scratched corners couch; there I sat, alone to face my powerlessness over wanting a drink, faced with flinging faith and God right out the front door like I would shoo a fly, as I shut myself in and shut the world out, me alone, for the night.

Only I had no wine in the house; none under the kitchen sink or on a shelf in the garage over the portable generator, just in case – a bottle of just-in-case behind a just-in-case generator. One never can know what one may need, just in case, the essentials, auxiliary power and a drink.

As it happened, just like the stories of those fortunate folks who answer the call to a purpose-driven life, I dutifully answered the call to mine. *Now*, I heard the voice within me shout, *if you run out to the corner store now, you'll return in time for the news and that happy-hour drink.*

Yesterday, on Groundhog Day, Punxsutawney Phil saw his shadow and crawled back into his sanctuary – six more weeks of winter ahead. In this southwestern high desert, six more weeks of drought, six more weeks of waiting for signs of spring, signs of hope, signs for raison d'être.

For me, in the sanctuary of my home, no shadow, no drought; I think I may have found my spark of divine, my alleluia in a glass of wine!

And now I've got a newly uncorked pinot noir under the sink. As I sit back and contemplate the long days of February still ahead, I ponder my options: Finish this drink, pour out the rest (hello?), restart my resolve, add makeup days to the end of the month, begin again tomorrow, February 4, because I've yet to make one day without a drink.

February 4

The loneliness begins. The long slog of loneliness begins. My husband (I'll call him Z and yes, I'm quite respectably married) Z left the house at four in the morning for a workweek in Utah. I am not new to his absences, or is it that his absences are not new to me? Last year he was away on work-related travel for a cumulative three months – four days here, one day there, five and ten and seven days and two. It all added up to three months away. Some by ground, some by air, some a combination of trains, planes and automobile; rentals, Uber and Lyft. Never by water. He can't swim.

This year marks our twentieth anniversary. A determined career woman from the time I fled my father Frank's house on Freedom Street, I had finally married because I promised my dying mother I would; otherwise, she claimed, she could never die in peace. Fearing for my future as an unmarried woman, she insisted that with her gone and me child-free and far from family, she insisted that I marry. *Marry*, she said. *You must marry*. When I insisted in return that there was no one out there for me, she would say: *Pick one, just pick one. I won't die until you marry.*

Thus I did. And thus she did soon thereafter. So I did pick one and marry. The pick – in the woo-woo weirdness of mystical matters – as I was then and to this day remain absolutely convinced, was my mother's pick for me.

On a hot October afternoon, after a leisurely hike along the foothills above orange and avocado orchards, in a village fifteen miles inland from the Pacific Ocean, 7,200 feet lower in elevation from here, where I lived a charmed life in a charming single-woman studio set among blooming pink oleanders, that hot first day of October, I strolled into the air-conditioned Hubba Hubba bar when lo and behold, there he stood, my mother's pick for me. There my man stood, the one I'd pick, my mother's pick for me. A tall drink of water, as they say, as the saying goes. Actually, being that I was in a bar, he was more like the straw that stands tall in the drink. Wrangler jeans, blue chambray shirt, Stetson hat and polished, pointy-toed boots – how could I not stake my claim?

Eight months later, we married. One month later, she died. She. My mother, my friend. The guiding light of my life went out like a star fallen from the sky. With whom would I share my news?

Naïve, immature, immortal, I never knew what loneliness was until I lost her. Almost a half-century old and her death left me hollowed out like a bomb-shelled crater. Despite these twenty years hence with a stand-in, a husband, I've never known again that kind of steady-eddy bosom-buddy kinship I had with her.

Thus, we married. Me, because I promised my mother. He? Well, I'm not sure why he married me, a woman ten years his senior. He could have married a woman ten years his junior; he could have had kids, even grandkids by now. Instead, he yoked himself to me.

What I was least prepared for in the years that have followed – we married on my mother's eighty-third birthday – was the ghostly presence of a third party. No, not a husband's ex-wife or debt or beer-drinking buddies nor fear of mistakes past. No, not the ghost of my mother. Yes, the ghost of my father and his legacy to me, the drink.

Marry we did and married we remain. The three of us: Z, me and the drink; we soldier on. Z's long absences and frequent career moves – we've moved eleven times up to this point – leave me in an everyday lonely, bereft without a familiar, comforting community, without lifelong friends nearby, without my mother. Looking back, which I try to avoid for all the heartache it gives me, I've left behind small towns, vibrant metros, careers and colleagues, favourite markets where I knew on which aisle to find the mayonnaise; hardware and second-hand stores; doctors and dentists, post offices, city halls, tree-lined avenues – the last, 9th Avenue, two blocks south of a university where I gave notice and kissed goodbye a wage that made me swoon.

Frequent moves in/out apartments, cabins, cottages and houses – my career now was to wear the mantle of homemaker, make each and every dwelling, however temporary, a home, because no sooner would I finally feel at home when it was time to pick up and move. I learned to make castles of all my homes in the manner of which my mother taught me: linens and lace, her mother's quilts, Shaker tablecloths and Amish cookware, always, her knitting needles rolled up into a tidy portable pocket-stitched keeper.

I knew but one home for the first eighteen years of my life, so all these subsequent moves could seem counterintuitive to what should have been my desire for home

– except over time I would prove that underneath the desire to find home and stay there, was a veiled urgency to flee, to be a fugitive from a past that pursued me like a pesky mosquito.

While all these moves were never my idea, I complied, as if tugged by a leash attached to a collar around my neck, pulled by an invisible master, answering to an urgency to flee, not just pack up and move, but to flee. Seems to this day I've never quite freed myself from the fight or flight response, ingrained, I would realise, in those first eighteen years of an unsparing home life.

With moving comes leaving, detaching, surrendering, blocking out the heartache of letting go, of saying goodbye, too many goodbyes, too many starting overs.

I've hardened myself to the leaving, learned to live with the dull deadness that comes from having to detach, from distancing, from walking away never to look back less I turn to stone. But I am, hard as stone when it comes to leaving. I could have been one of those pioneer women in a covered wagon; not only did she give up her family, her genteel sensibilities, but she risked leaving keepsakes, small and large, along the side of the road.

My keepsakes left behind range from an antique, cane-seat rocking chair (I'd soaked and woven the reeds myself), a rustic pine bureau, boxes of books, boxes of dishes and kitsch; pottery, yard art of willow trellises and iron gates. Most mourned, I've left behind immovables, irreplaceables: my gardens.

Gardens. Nothing roots one more securely to their homestead than their gardens: heirloom tomatoes, leaf lettuce, peppers, squash. I learned to cultivate a home as I did my gardens, all in the manner in which my mother taught me. Not just vegetables, but roses, wisteria, red-twigged dogwood, purple crocus and evening primrose. I so miss the stark beauty of the leggy red-twigs, contrasting like a painter's bold strokes against white snow. Beauty and bounty, I started from scratch but left behind for someone else to enjoy, or not. Our tastes may not have been the same.

Places, people, things – I've come to love but also came to grieve. For all of these moves, I've abandoned writers' groups, chiropractors, hairdressers, farmers' markets, treasured places, people and things, never to be enjoyed again.

For all of Z's absences, I think I could have gotten away with hooking up with another man. Finding a filler fellow. I almost had myself one once. He was a preacher, handsome and passionate, not just about Jesus, but also about me. Thought I would make a good preacher's wife. Are you kidding? Scared me enough to run for cover, enough never to stare googly-eyed at another man again. Swore off even the slightest suggestion to flirt, to engage, because I don't like messy; I like things neat, orderly, predictable and calm. No filler fellow needed to help me through these long absences, the loneliness, the hollowness in my core. Instead, I've fallen for the comfort and company of that aforementioned third party: The drink.

Last night, I put away yet another empty wine bottle, casually dropped it bottom first into the blue recycle bin. At the moment, I have no wine in the house whatsoever. There are a few beers in the refrigerator, Z's drink of choice, but I'm not usually tempted to pop open one of those. I can leave beer alone and the number of pints on the top shelf as of this writing will be the same number when Z returns.

I am not an alcoholic. No one has ever suggested such, least not in my earshot; of course, I sense my hearing slipping too. Z says I don't have a problem. In fact, he's the one who keeps me in stock, stopping at the corner market on his way home from work to buy me another. He'll even uncork it for me, set it on the counter to breathe before he sits down to his salad. The wine breathes and so do I.

Those evenings, I'll pour a short snort and he'll grab a beer and we'll sit at the table to look at each other; he, over the top of the newspaper; me, out the window into the black of the night. Sometimes one of us has something to say. I'm reminded of a movie, *The Phantom Thread*, where Reynolds and Alma sit at the table and stare at each other in silence while dreary background music monotonously drones on.

I rarely refill my glass those evenings because it's already late and I'm tired and, now that the bottle is open, I want to have it for myself, to hoard and savour while he's away, over the coming days of his absence. I may have mentioned, I can make a bottle last for at least three days. I know my limits, when I can and when I should not, pour myself another. Does Z really know how much I drink? I think he does. Do I know how much I drink? Yes.

Here's where I stand: today, day four, I restart my month of February all over again, albeit abridged to an even shorter month of twenty-four days, because I screwed up days one, two and three. I renew my vow to abstain from alcohol at least until the end of this month. Do you follow? I start my goal to abstain from alcohol to test myself, to see if I can and for reasons I've always wanted to stop the flow: financial (could save thousands); calories (could save many thousands – although I'm already skinny). Maybe the quality of my sleep would improve and maybe my memory would improve. But what's to remember?

This week I'll be facing loneliness twofold: for my husband's absence and for the absence of a drink. I like them both, enjoy their company, feel less restless when they're around.

This day and for the rest of this abridged month, I'll once again vow to abstain.

Two hours have passed since last I wrote. It's Sunday morning, I've got another two hours before this state's liquor laws allow for sales. When we first moved here, before I knew *the law*, one Sunday morning, when I was about to set a bottle in my cart, the manager just so happened to be walking by. *You can't buy that now*, he snapped. Still choking the illicit item by the neck, I looked up at him and before I could utter a why, he barked, *It's the law. No liquor sales on Sunday before noon.* I was a bit embarrassed, not for lack of knowledge for the law, but because he may have assumed I would drink before noon. Not that that hasn't ever happened.

Which reminds me of a study that claims folks who drink more than seven a week can expect to die sooner than those who drink less. Well, I'll wait on the study to come out that refutes that claim. Besides, why would I give up the drink for a longer life, when it's the drink that gives me a life to live?

Busy, get busy, start ticking off the chores on my to-do list: wipe down the ceiling fan blades, change out the sheets (Z likes flannel; me, percale), wash the sheets, hang the sheets on the line to dry – yes, it's February, but unseasonably warm, nice enough to hang the sheets out to dry – put the sheets back on the bed; pay bills, take out the shower buckets of water, weed, whack a gopher over his head; read another few paragraphs from David Brooks, read a passage from Richard Rohr; find the last end piece to complete the frame to the jigsaw puzzle I set up on a folding table in the bedroom; set out the sewing machine to take in the waist of my pants, knit another hat, finish applying a beeswax oil to the kitchen cabinets. Always, always, daily, twice a day, come hell or high water, come gale-force winds that sandblast my face, take the dog for a walk. Vacuum, dust, mop, scrub, yada, yada, yada. Buff out my husband's bathroom. This tiny house came blessed with two tiny bathrooms. I wait for Z to leave to thoroughly clean his. There's nothing worse than cleaning a man's bathroom.

And work on reviving my vocabulary. Knead those depleting brain cells, proof them like yeast into regeneration. Tied for the *there's nothing worse than* category, of cleaning a man's bathroom, there's nothing worse than wading through a book written by an erudite author who uses smart words I can neither pronounce nor interpret their meaning. There was a time when I could, but not these days.

February 5

So, who am I without the drink? And what would an abstinence tell me? Will I notice change that I would want to make permanent? Will any change matter? What if I like myself just the way I am, drink and all?

I think that's the essence to this experiment. To test my mettle, to find out just who I am, what I'm made of, to test a self-devised hypothesis using yours truly on both sides of the control groups: *Participants were divided into two categories: those who continued to imbibe on their routine, habitual basis and those who completely abstained for a month.* It's curious if results will show, for those who abstained, a difference in several measurements: social behaviour, food choice, sleep, weight loss or gain, memory, an improvement to eyesight, a relief from joint pain, a renewed energy and perhaps even a reprieve on paranoia and loneliness. And so long forgotten, what I wouldn't give for a little fire in the belly.

About those measurements.

Social behaviour? Having learned to become accustomed to my own company, likable or not, I prefer to drink alone. I'd just as soon be alone, be left alone, just like the abandoned child I've subconsciously believed myself to be. I've lost my touch for acceptable social behaviour, behaviour that was way too hard to learn after growing up those eighteen years in that awkward home. Perhaps due to my aloneness, I've lost my touch for what's proper talk in a group – which is to suggest I ever practised socially acceptable behaviours, because in our house, what was proper was at the same time, well, never quite proper. These days, I'm out of my comfort zone when out of the house, when forced to dress out of the uniform of my own skin.

Food choice? Aside from never knowing whether the mashed potatoes or borscht would be served at the table or scraped from a wall, we ate what came from the garden, what was baked in the oven, what came up from the basement from barrels brimming with sauerkraut and cured meats. Beans, beets, carrots, corn, cucumbers, onions, peas, potatoes; everything we ate we harvested from our gardens. Every autumn my mother and her little helpers laboured and sweated over kettles of boiling hot water, a monster of a pressure cooker, baskets of ripened garden vegetables that we washed, sorted, cut up and put up in gleaming quart jars, labelling, dating and lining them along cold cellar walls of sagging shelves.

Besides produce, we kept chickens. Who wouldn't want to sit down to bowls of fresh killed, gutted and plucked, steaming chicken soup, feet and neck, gizzard, liver and heart, parts-unknown-soup with boiled vegetables and homemade thick egg noodles? I'd say that was pretty healthy stuff, except for the occasional too much salt. All of which, as a grownup I can vouch, goes great with pinot noir. 'Course, Frank would enjoy his cellar-brewed beer, or, on occasion, a Mason jar of elderberry mash. Sure, my tastes have evolved – none of that sour mash. It's store-bought, vineyard quality, pinot noir for me.

Whoa there! Slow down the preachy crap. *Save me, O Jesus, from myself,* not from the drink, that holy wedding-blessed water-to-wine miraculously produced at Cana. Wasn't your message that we shouldn't wait for later to bring out the best? Or am I confusing that with a catchy Hellman's mayonnaise television jingle? Isn't every day a reason one rises from the litter, if not to raise a glass?

Sleep? They say that drink's a downer, destructive to a good night's rest. Sure, one may go out as soon as the head drops, but then the duration and quality of sleep may suffer. Suffer. Let me interject here. I think it's possible that I have become accustomed to suffering, to the point of longsuffering, wearing it invisibly emblazoned on my chest like an early Christian martyr.

My fix for sleeplessness and longsuffering, is to drink earlier in the day, be done with it hours before it's time to pull down the shades. I'm not a night drinker; I begin early enough in the day (and I'm not confessing to before noon) to make it last. By the time an evening comes to its end, when I've run out of pinot noir, when my longsuffering ebbs, I'm ready to drift to sleep on fumes.

Still, insomnia persists. I'm not convinced the drink has the upper hand on my inability to rest in slumber and I'm rather fervent in the belief that a month of abstinence will not likely improve my sleep. Forget about pills; if it's a sedative I could pop to chase the sleep thieves away, I'd sooner choose the drink. Better, I'd sooner choose to cast out the demons, if only they would leave.

Weight loss or gain? My clothes hang on me like Spanish moss from trees. A work colleague once remarked: *Your clothes are too big, did something happen to you when you were a kid?* First of all, the fourth child from the top, mine were genderless hand-me-downs: coats, dresses, even my brother's shoes. Secondly, for whatever happened that may support her inference, for the record, I like my clothes loose, makes me feel small and slight, yes, invisible, underneath and within the folds of so much material – a lot like the capacious (new word!) heavy black polyester habits worn by the Dominican nuns of my Catholic school days – plays into my comfort in not being seen, plays into a cloaked need to feel wrapped in love.

Memory? It's a guess whether I destroy brain cells associated with memory, but then again, what would I be doing with an excess anyway? Learning something new? I feel burdened with what I already studied so hard to learn, what I strived and saved all my money for: to get an education, to get smart, to amount to more than what Frank drunkenly, unforgivably pounded and drummed into my head: *You'll never amount to nothing. You hear me? You're just no good, a good for nothin'!*

And where did those degrees get me but another degree of unworthiness for not being better or smarter or richer, or what the hell, even marrying higher up, not that Z, at six-foot-three, isn't above average? I could've easily smothered myself to death from under the crush of all those books, for all that learning, for all the nothing I've predictably become, despite achieving honours status. Instead I suffer in silent self-rebuke, Marlin Brando's sorry line, *I coulda been a contender,* ringing between my ears like a church bell.

I know for fact I'm losing memory, but is this drink or age related? – have I broached this subject before? I have a feeling we've had this conversation before. Last week? Yesterday maybe? Or earlier today? Oh well, excuse me as I repeat myself, that I forget what I've said before. I'm often at a loss for memory for a birthday or a name or event. That's why I make notes; they're ubiquitous as dog hairs, scraps of paper with notes to remind me what to buy at the store, what I want to tell Z when he comes home, what to add to the never-ending to-do list of outdoor chores and domestic activity. These days, things related to memory orbit 'round my head like stars after a good clunk. Sometimes I'm lucky to pluck a memory like a plum from the tree right when I need it, but most times I lose them forever to a puff and it's gone! I like to think that a memory lost will one day resurface and then I can have an aha! But I don't count on that. It gets easier to give way to memory crashes with each passing day.

As for memory lost to a drink, well, that could be, but I have no way of knowing, no way to test, no evidence to prove, that my hiccups in memory are connected to the drink. None whatsoever, as I recall.

Eyesight? If I knew for sure that abstinence from drink would improve my vision, could even curtail or reverse my glaucomic condition, of course I would drain that bottle immediately – hold on there, but not necessarily down the sink. Now let's just take this slowly. Allow me to finish what I've started. But I've yet to come across any empirical evidence that abstinence relieves the symptoms of glaucoma or could even reverse what has been lost. Hmm. Reverse what has been lost. As if a drink could help with that.

As for joint pain? Just keep moving, I tell myself. Just keep moving. Set aside a short snort of drink nearby and just keep moving.

At this juncture, I may have lost you, dear reader; I confess I've lost myself, as I meander between the paradoxes of reality, subtexts and stream of consciousness babble and brooding over the consequences and benefits, of a drink. I haven't even touched upon my thoughts on the measurements of abstinence with regards to renewed energy, a reprieve from paranoia and loneliness. And what was so vital about wanting to feel fire in the belly anyway? I suffer from burnout enough! Listen to me, back to suffering. I can't live without my lifelong companion and friend, longsuffering.

It's later, towards the end of my day. I've resisted temptation to pour a drink, despite this being Super Bowl Sunday, when America pours herself a drink. When Z is away, I play the TV loud, to hear from every empty room, up and down the empty corridor that connects them all.

Thus I've managed to begin – to have a day one – yesterday, on day four; and for today, this day five of February, as I pull down the shades and bring my day to a close, I may actually succeed in making this day two, without the drink.

February 6

I survived day two without the drink.

I've thought more about the *what* and *why* for both abstaining from the drink and then writing about the experiment.

During a rare telephone conversation with a friend I confessed to her this project. I wanted to get feedback on the worthiness of the endeavour, because this early on, I was tempted to quit. But she surprised me and volunteered to read and give feedback on my entries. We'd met decades ago on a university campus in California; she was an unregistered student, but a gifted one, so the instructors let her sit in. Come to find out we lived on the same country road within a mile of each other! One stormy, relentlessly rainy day a torrential flood ripped through the canyons and took away my home, bits and pieces of the whole of my life up to that event were strewn all the way to the ocean. In the aftermath, she came and pulled pyjamas and panties, shirts and jeans from the mud and took them home to launder.

Some people do things to fulfil a sense of purpose, to live out what they feel sure is their destiny. Some people do things because they can't help themselves; they can't stop themselves from doing whatever it is they are doing, things which could be detrimental or derelict or dangerous to themselves or others, bad things that could drive them to escape through drink; dark things they may have done in the past, dark and haunting for which there is no escape but the drink. Or situations could exist that dark things happened to them from which they must forever run, or turn to the drink.

Now I can't speak for anyone but myself and even then, I'm never quite sure for what it is I think I may know. However, I know my predilections, even what's inherent to me, like the inherent predilection for the drink. It's in the family, all in the family, an inherited, inherent need and predilection for, the drink. And yes, it's a need, more demanding than a preference, although, as I said, mine is pinot noir. My inherent need for the drink just so happens to correspond to a dereliction in predilection which then prompts the elbow to extend and the hand to reach, for the bottle under the sink. I can't say exactly what sets the prompt in motion; it's as though whole-body directed, to pull the trigger and once the bullet leaves the barrel, well, the deed is done.

Let's get it straight, I'm talking to myself here, trying to explain to myself here. About abstaining. I'm trying to go an abridged month – forget that I missed the start date for February, just go with me on the newly revised goal for twenty-four days without a drink and I don't know if I can, for whatever benefits I may reap. Can I do it? Do I have the discipline? Will I be a better person for it? Will my health improve? Will I lose the bags under my eyes, the hopelessness in my heart? Will I plug the drain to keep those brain cells that remain from drowning in the drink? Will I save my soul?

About the writing. What I want to get down is how hard it is to will myself away from the drink, how hard my struggle to divert myself away from the path I seem meant to take. No matter the distractions intended to keep my mind and hand off the drink, all paths lead back to the bottle under the sink. As I sense myself drifting towards the cabinet, I find my thoughts drifting away from any and all good reasons to quit, even for twenty-eight days, or is that now twenty-four? Nobody's telling me to quit, advising that I quit; heck, nobody notices much about me to begin with, except that maybe my clothes are too big.

Yesterday, mid-afternoon, I almost had to super-glue myself to a chair to keep from running out the door for a new bottle of wine. By early evening, I was ready to reach for one of Z's beers.

That storm passed without catastrophe. When I'm alone in this house save for the dog and the cat and the television and my many to-do lists, lists I treasure like interest-bearing bank notes, lists that float from room to room like dust bunnies, I steel myself against temptation and force myself to focus on my lists. Until I fold like an ironing board.

Mine is a sparsely populated neighbourhood, if one could even call it such, where on any given morning I can count more coyotes than humans. Earlier, before coffee and quiet time to sit and write (I'm enshrouded in quiet time! Would that I could bottle time in those empty bottles of wine and sell them online!) I went outside in this unseasonably dry winter in wildly blowing wind to water, to quench the parched piñons and junipers, miscellaneous shrubs that remarkably survive the drought and desert critters.

Filling buckets at the kitchen sink, I ferried gallons through the open back door to offer relief to cat mint, Virginia creepers, boxwoods, three purple invasive Russian sages I started from cuttings with hopes they would take root and well, invade. In this case, I invite the Russian (sage) invasion; they are welcome here as long as they bring the vodka.

In the process of watering, I also build up my upper body strength and firm those triceps that can hang down like sideways sails on a woman my age. I lift and carry and walk hundreds of steps, no, tens of thousands would total at the end of the day, with buckets and buckets of water from sink to unfrozen ground. Only I just recently learned that, like yoga, I should refrain from strain if I want to preserve my vision, so no more five-gallon lifts. Instead, I do half buckets and make more trips. I think I may have mentioned this already.

If I knew conclusively that abstinence (referring to the drink here) would positively for the better affect my glaucoma, I would quit forever at the snap of a towel and I would quit this diary of a drink right now. Instead of wasting away with a bottle and this blah-blah, I would jump in the car and drive myself to my favourite charity, an Indian casino.

Which brings me to say something more about the necessity and my propensity for, distractions. These include reading while my eyes can distinguish a *c* from an *e* and an *i* from an *l*; knitting while my eyes can discern a dropped stitch; picking over jigsaw pieces to find a fit; hanging laundry out in the wind before it gets so strong it whips the sheets into knots, or worse, they fly airborne into the arroyo; walking the dog, watching reruns of *Murder She Wrote* (while I knit), oiling kitchen cabinet hardware – don't want the wine cubby to tell on me – cleaning the dust and applying beeswax to the wood window casings, wiping down the dust, daily, wiping down and up the dust, from table tops to ceiling fans, baseboards and lampshades. Did I mention we live on a dirt road, a dusty, finely pulverised clay-dirt road? When a Fed-Ex truck rumbles by, it leaves a mushroom cloud as broad as a city block. Yes, I probably mentioned the aforesaid.

When Z is away, I indulge in both watching TV and in long-distance telephone conversations with girlfriends left behind: in California, up and down the coast, along the Western and Eastern Sierras; in Colorado, Idaho, Ohio, Utah, Montana, Washington State, Upstate New York and an outlier in Alabama. These women are like AA sponsors to me, at the ready to listen to what I may have to say, but I rarely do share my details as I'd rather sit quietly and listen to them. Of course, they don't know it, they don't know I'm writing this diary of a drink (except my lone reader); they don't suspect that I think I have an issue with the drink. But then, neither do I! Actually, the outlier in Alabama is my lone reader. She divides her retirement between California and Alabama. In our latest conversation, she confessed she misplaced pages of this diary, not sure in which state she left them. Of course, I would email the pages she's missing but she's old school, doesn't text or email, depends on snail mail to deliver my envelopes. But to avoid any do-overs, I told her to never mind, it wasn't that important and what she shares with me over the phone will be sufficient enough. I give my long-distance friends credit for hanging in there with me because, left to my own dysfunction-abilities, well, I've been known to simply move on without a trace.

It's occurring to me as I type how small my world is, inside this small pueblo revival sand-stuccoed dwelling, within this small community, restricted by my limited eyesight. When Z is away, I hardly get out, as I am his Miss Daisy to his Hoke. I have access to a car, but it's really the dog's car; it's parked alongside a fence, available to me in case of emergency, like when I run out of wine.

And yes, I can legally drive, insomuch as I passed the test three years ago. But safety is another matter. I can drive a mile to the corner store on a stretch of surface roads, plus I can drive a mile in another direction to the waste transfer station to deposit trash and recycles. And I can drive a mile in a third direction to where a group of women meet once a week to knit, share project ideas and news. I learn a lot from these women, about how to long-tail cast on, about how much bigger their houses are than mine, with their portals and walled-in courtyards, their studio guest casitas; about spinning and dyeing wool sheared from their alpacas, about their smart, almost driverless cars; their smart doctor sons. When I arrive at the meeting room, I take a fabric-covered winged chair across from the cushy leather couches on which they rest their soft thighs of retirement. There I can sit and observe, knit and listen and reflect on how small my world is, my house, my income, even my interests and how, perhaps not unlike other lonely people, I try to make-believe it's not important, try to pretend I don't feel a modicum of envy for their lives so successfully lived.

It's nearly seven in the morning. I've been up out of bed since four. At daylight, I went out and watered more plants and shrubs, thereafter walked the dog. Tick off the watering, but not the dog. I'll take her out again around noon. I'm a morning person. I start my day in the dark and pretty much end it by late afternoon. Last night I tossed and turned, slept so poorly and restlessly that it's a wonder I can function at all today. But I do, zombie-like that I do. I got up and started my day pleased with myself I made it to another day, is this day two or three? without the drink.

Already I fret whether I'll have the strength and stamina to make it through this day. A long stretch of hours lay ahead. Better get busy on those lists. But oh! How a glass of wine would ease the boredom, lift the boredom of domestic activity to tackle in the hours ahead. Please, if you really knew me, knew me when, knew me from who I was, compared me to who I am today, you might understand that while my life as I write it today may seem boring and trite, you would have never called me boring back when; when those women friends (not the knitters) I wrote about earlier knew me back when. If you happen to be my age, happen to have lived through experiences you could never relive today, because you've aged out, because the prime of your life has slipped by, because you no longer have the energy it takes for anything, much less live, however so gently or not, then you would understand what boredom and loneliness is to some of us today. But it's not that we missed out, on what was once a big life back when. It's not that we don't remember how it once all was. For how big our lives were then, once upon a time. Memory for what once was. It's a two-sided blade that cuts either way, painful yet sweet, but of little relevance today.

February 7

3:20 a.m. I knew it was 3:20 even before I put my feet on the floor to go write this down. Of course, I can't sleep. Why would I think that if I abstain from the drink, if I get fresh air and exercise during the day, that if I don't eat anything that is a known sleep-stopper before I go to bed, that if I feel satisfied enough for how I spent the day, that if I've read and gleaned from Brooks and Rohr the spiritual wisdom they write to impart, if I've prayed in petition for all those who suffer, from disease and war, the migrants and refugees, victims of the world politic knocking on heaven's door; if I've prayed in thanksgiving for my own blessings aplenty; what with ticking off the chores on my lists and fighting with every punch I can muster to pulverize those demons that plague me like gnats all during the day, so why do I expect to lay my head on a pillow and sleep?

It cannot be the drink that wrecks my sleep. It just makes no sense, the randomness of sleep, the randomness of anything! It's in those long and woeful wee hours of the night when I find myself in that dark place where I just know it has to be me, the essence of *me* that keeps me from sleep. It's my life. It's who I am. It's how God made me. Who made me? God made me. Why did God make me? God only knows.

It's how I was made, how I was formed from the clay of the earth, the contaminants that were in that clay; how I was raised, like a cornstalk in the field or like a cow in the pasture, cultivated and raised up by the farmer who expects his fields and cows to prosper and yield. Because he's been led by some false expectations that if he does it right, he will prosper, too. If I do it right, if I'm good, if I follow the rules of the *Thou Shall Nots,* then I shall prosper, too. Not. I will sleep because I'm good and follow the rules. Not.

I can't sleep because I can't sleep. I can't weep. I have a friend, the one who had the eyelid lift, who cries every day; she weeps like a wound that won't heal. She's lucky. I had a good cry a couple years ago when we buried our beloved cat, Boots, under the Juniper and before that, eighteen years in fact, when I buried my mother up on a hill in our hometown in Ohio. *Point my feet towards the shopping centre,* she specified, *I want to watch the people.* God knows she was lonely too.

It's how I learned to live when I was raised, no, not learned, yes, learned, how I learned to adapt to get any amount of sleep before Frank lit up. It's that scrap-heap of a family onto which I was slung. It's my Maker's cruel joke: *Here, let's put you with these folks here, you cute little clueless bugger. Let's see how you manage to grow and prosper here, with this thug of a man and miserably misguided woman, this rat pack of outcasts they are doomed to hatch and unleash. Let's see you Houdini yourself out of this. I'll sit back and enjoy the show.* How can we call him a loving God when he smirks at his own cruel jokes?

It's everything I can't cope with as a result of who I am and the so-called family I came from and the God-forsaken curse upon me when delivered to those people, that house on Freedom Street and that curse.

It's all the choices I have made and continue to make because I'm running as fast as I can; no, I don't run anymore, I plod. I just can't cope. With or without the drink. What's this experiment for, to drink, or not to drink, except to confirm what I already know? And just what do I know? And what do I do with what I know?

After a hot cup of filtered water with fresh-squeezed lemon juice (Meyer lemons sent from my reader who just so happens to be at this time in California) and a big spoon of honey (a friend's bee boxes in Idaho), a quick read of a book review of Erica Garza's *Getting Off*, I plodded back to bed, taking David Brooks with me. I remember hearing the book hit the floor which woke me enough to push the tip of the cat's tail away from my nose. I remember hearing my cell phone chime from where I left it in the kitchen, guessing correctly it was Z, checking in, messaging a *good morning* from wherever he laid his head on a hotel pillow his night before.

February 8

This morning I made it to 3:35 a.m. Although I flipped all night like a fish out of water, I'm not as edgy. It's awful to wake up edgy. The first noise, disturbance, or bump into a door or drawer can set me off for the rest of the day and that's a bad beginning for a morning person like me.

Fish out of water. Maybe that's what I am. Maybe I'm not all that odd, just a fish out of water that jumped the pail and flops on the pier, waiting, just hoping, that someone (God? Myself?) will show mercy and throw me back into the safe confines of a bucket. Better, they toss me over the railing into the sea. I'm already confined in a bucket of a life as it is, in this desert, this wind, these dusty roads, the pebbles in my shoes, all this dust kicked up by cars – inconsiderate UPS and Fed-Ex drivers who go too fast and spew dust in my eyes, the grit that gets through my lips, the grit in my mouth between my teeth. Or maybe I just go too slow.

Oh, how I miss the ocean; how I miss the fog and the early morning walks on hard-packed sand at low tide. When I lived at the beach, I would wake to the foghorn, dress and walk before sunrise along the brink of foamy ocean water, north to the pier, then south to the beached and boulder-buried party boat, the La Janelle, if I remember correctly her name.

Already, 4:11 a.m. The house is quiet; pets are fed. The dog went back to her lair under my desk and the cat, having begged me beyond my patience – meow, meow, meow, MEOW! – to go out, lies in wait under a stack of two-by-fours laid like planks between sawhorses next to the shed, a blue tarp over, under which he can hunker, watch and wait, for a mouse to come out for him to pounce. I'll go check on him now, bring him inside, because early mornings like this make me wary a coyote will jump the fence and pounce on my cat.

When I walked outside to check on the cat, despite my poor eyesight – so bright and beautiful the stars here, they hang low like ripe fruit – I walked right onto the spoon of the big dipper, as if God and not a coyote, was waiting to scoop me up to heaven.

A cup of coffee sits at my right. Hah! And you suspected it might be wine! A revised list of treasury notes (a.k.a. chores) on my left. Plus a new word, *sententious*, scratched on a note pad at the bottom of a growing collection of words whose meanings I must look up, words I don't use in my everyday vocabulary because I've become more of a commoner since leaving the workplace, the classroom, since leaving klatches of kindred writers in whose manuscripts I would discover such words, these recently come-upon words I circle in pencil when I read to remind myself to look them up. I scribbled *sententious* under *pogrom*. Have I mentioned this list (note: a non-chore list) of words I'm compiling to learn? For some to relearn? Because while I may sense a memory for that word, I cannot be sure. I can never be sure. What is it about aging that makes me unsure of so much of which I once was most certainly sure?

Yes, in my readings, I stumble onto words unfamiliar to me or for whose meaning I may have known in an earlier life – I'll throw out here I may very well be on life number eight of nine, if I can borrow from the cat – but can remember no longer, a bit like friends I've known and forgotten, places I've lived and forgotten too. It's probably a blessing to forget, friends and homes, people and places, because remembering can be so sad.

Some of these words I can neither pronounce nor try to interpret their meaning as used in the context of the sentence, the paragraph, the narrative. I do take the time to look them up, these words no longer friends of mine. In fact, I go back in time to the old school way, lug from the bottom shelf of a nearby bookcase and open on the floor my heavy hardbound desk dictionary – *American Heritage*, Third Edition – I look the mystery words up in a print edition of a now extinct dinosaur dictionary, a once time-honoured exercise in body and mind. Still, an exercise in body and mind for me.

Yesterday, I couldn't write much because I couldn't sort things churning inside my head, like those bingo balls bouncing off the sides of a hand-crank clear plastic bin. But this is where the chore lists come in. After sitting down at the table with pen, paper – usually the back side of a junk-mail envelope – to sort out my thoughts and revise, rewrite my lists, I start to feel better, like maybe I've got something accomplished? Like maybe a wee bit of order begins to take shape? Like maybe I could really shake off the hangover that can hover all day after a sleepless night, yes, not dissimilar to the hangover from too much drink?

Maybe I can attribute the sleepless hangover to the ice cream I spoon-fed myself before I went to bed. It's

46

compensation, you know, a half-pint of ice cream instead of a half-pint of drink. Too much sugar can give me a hangover the next day. Sometimes I'll have the glass of wine and then the dessert. But for every sip, for every spoonful, I worry about damage, the stuff that can kill me, or worse, can cause me pain – I don't do well with pain, but I do great with suffering – God spare me the pain of suffering, from the pain associated with disease, diabetes, liver failure. I wonder if one feels pain with dementia.

My younger brother suffers from the pain and consequences of diabetes – they want to take off his left foot and from there, you know they'll go right up the leg. My youngest sister is in renal failure. She was warned about this a year ago but did not act. In a renewed effort to encourage my sister to get treatment, the doctor asked her if she had something she wanted to do, meaning, a reason to live. She said yes; if asked of me, I would say no. No, there's nothing much I want to do. Except sleep. Not much reason to live, except I would welcome one good night's sleep, not the long rest into eternity, just a one-nighter, an intoxicatingly delicious sleep, a new next morning, not like the one I woke up to today. I live for a new day to experience what it's like to have had a good night's sleep. No, there's nothing much I want to do, certainly not compared to my lists of what I seem to think I have to do. Not much reason to live, yet I do. And *yes*, I tell my sister, *that's my blood type too* and *yes; I'll give a kidney to you.*

This, by the by, is the sister who doesn't touch the stuff, the drink, and she's the one with a disease common to the drink! It's only right I give her one of mine, a kidney that is, as if, I'm assuming, I have a healthy one to share.

Last night I dreamed in animation and in colour. I had come across an eight-page spread on the Turks & Caicos Islands in the Caribbean. It was inside a May 2010 *National Geographic* magazine. It's been years since I've yearned to travel anywhere on such a vacation as that, what with all the chaos at airports, lines through TSP, oh, wait, or is it TSA? body scans, claustrophobic, suffocating airplanes with an oversize sick person sitting in the seat next, their therapy dog in a carry-on taking its last breath in an overhead bin, but last night, in my dreams, after seeing the vivid blue-green waters and golden beaches, feeling the warm breeze lift the hair on my bare arms, I felt the desire for pleasures of travel well up inside me like I had just stumbled onto the opium-induced poem by Coleridge, the mystical *Kubla Kan*. In this dream, I shared the magazine pages, open to the pictures, with a friend, suggesting to her that she should go. That's just like me, to give away my fun, to abandon my dreams. It's been so long, I hardly remember I once had either: real-life dreams, ordinary fun. I'd probably clasp my hand over my fluttering heart, collapse in a last breath, die on the spot, should any fun be extra-ordinary again.

Oh, as well, I dreamed I flushed a toilet, but the poo would not go down; there was too much for it all to flush down. Is that a metaphor for my life, too much shit, really, the unrealistic struggle to flush it all down, the wad of gummy distractions, items on the lists, the evacuation I seek from this crap load of a life? I can see where the metaphors could really pile on.

At least this morning I did not wake up to the paranoia that hijacked me the day before. I can't understand where that comes from, but I understand the why. Paranoia – she extracts the juices out of me like a blender whirling on high.

When paranoia sets in, I fight off thoughts of how wretched I am, how everything that goes wrong is my fault, that I'm stupid and careless and lacking the social skills of a crab. And then I start to think I'm just like Frank. There can't be anything worse than thinking that I'm just like Frank. Or his sister, my Aunt Lucille, who in her old age thought the CIA had tapped her telephone and she could not talk into it for fear they would hear something they had been waiting for her to say and then they would come get her and take her away. I don't fear that anyone will come to take me away and I don't ever fear I will cause myself harm, because, as I've said, I don't like pain.

My chore list today looks much the same as it did two days ago, despite the revisions. I've managed to clean the ceiling fan blades from the fixture over the bed, got up and dusted and unscrewed the ceramic hoods that house the bulbs, removed the bulbs and wiped them clean. They're sitting on the bureau waiting to go back in. Maybe today I'll wrap that task up.

Twice I've brought out the step-stool from the garage to finish wiping down the upper kitchen cabinets and twice I've put it away to get it out of the way. Maybe I'll listen to a radio program this morning while the sun comes up through the kitchen windows and light shines on the pine doors while I clean and light shines on me. That should brighten my spirits and my day.

And I've decided not to shorten that ankle-length robe so I will not drag out the sewing machine to stitch a hem and I've returned my very special dressmaking scissors back to their box, from when I got them out to cut the robe short in the first place. But I did set out the two socks with holes in the toes for me to mend on the table in front of the couch. I just have to pick through my darning thread, rather, I prefer yarn, for a colour that won't match – I don't like things to match – get a needle and use a green avocado to push into the toe, turn on the television for company and mend. I like to darn socks. My mother would sit under a floor lamp in the evenings when we all anxiously awaited a long overdue Frank, bring out her sewing basket and darn our socks. Now I just have to find *Little House on the Prairie* to watch while I mend. I'll sneak in here how much the television, no matter the programming, repetitive sales pitches, latest big pharma drug fixes, no matter the loud and blatant intrusion it is in my living room, no matter the clatter, the chatter, the boredom, the insult to my intelligence, why, it's company I welcome nevertheless.

For sure, I won't get to Z's bathroom until Friday. When he returns Friday evening he'll walk into a newly minted bathroom, sink, toilet, shower, floors, faucets, a freshly laundered, outdoor line-dried stiff and scratchy towel, just the way he likes it.

Out of the blue – here it's blue sky, no trees to block, we have plenty of blue sky, but I wish it were blue water instead – out of the blue my phone rang from a caller in Idaho. I didn't recognise the number – no name came across the screen – but I knew the area code was Idaho, so I answered, because it was Idaho and I welcomed a call and possible dialogue with someone I knew from a life before, from when I had a life and friends and home in Idaho.

Hello? It's Mick. And then it clicked in my head who Mick was and we proceeded to have a conversation, which was basically about my coming back to work. After a bit of jostling with jokes and recollections for the capital improvement project we worked together on back then, he asked me to consider that I do it again, only from where I am, not from where he is, from where I used to be and he asked me to sleep on it and at the moment I can't think how my dreams of the Turks and Caicos could possibly fit in with that call, but I thought about the conversation all day, tried to think how I could possibly do that job again from where I live now, but what really prevailed were thoughts about moving back there again, leaving this lonely and almost pointless existence that brings me little joy and satisfaction and going back to one more fulfilling as it was back then. As it was back then. Somehow, I have sense enough to realise I could never return to anything from an *as it was back then*. As if that would validate the who that I now am; as if by saying yes, I would receive a stamp of approval across my forehead. *No thank you, Mick, I don't have it in me to go back to a way back when, as it was back then.* I somewhat said.

It's just after five. I'm going to take a break, leave the page and begin my day in fact. Nuke my coffee and rehash in my head what I've written and think, think, think about what it is I'm trying to get straight in my head, about anything and everything and nothing.

After five. In the morning, that is. I should try to go back to bed, try to behave like a normal human being and get some sleep, unclench these jaws. I could also mend those socks, read from Brooks or Rohr, or possibly make breakfast, but it's too early for food. If only it were light outside, if only I could find the courage to drive, despite this damned glaucoma, if only I would feel confident enough not to jeopardise the safety of anyone else, I would get in my car and take the dog and head out for…for what? And where would I go and for what?

February 9

Better. It's five in the morning – could've started earlier, but I made myself stay in bed in the dark with the covers pulled over my head.

My cat goes to the vet at 7:30. He's screaming at me from the other side of the closed door to this, a small room in the back of this small house, I use for an office, junk catch-all. It occurs to me how small my world has become, or have I said this before? How rooms and even my body continue to shrink, perhaps in proportion to how glaucoma shrinks my vision, how my brain must shrink too.

Poor kitty; he's screaming! He wants food. Feed Me! Feed Me! *I can't feed you, oh, I'm so sorry, I can't feed you; you're not allowed food. I have to take you to the vet for a teeth cleaning and possible extractions and they will have to sedate you!* Oh, Lord, I wish I could sedate him now! Him? Me! Oh, Lord, I wish I could sedate me! Poor kitty. When I shuffled into the kitchen just after five in the morning to turn on the coffee, he leaped up on a chair and sat on the edge and just glared at me through tightly squinted eyes, screaming, waiting for me to pop the top to his can of gravy Fancy Feast; screamed while I scooped out the dog's hearty turkey stew.

No, I can't even let you lick the spoon my kitty kitty. I am so sorry. I am so sorry. Let me list the ways.

That I am so sorry. What a way to begin a day, with a screaming cat and a screaming headache! That's probably from making myself stay in bed. You can get a headache from making yourself do things you really don't want to do, you know, like staying in bed to help pass time and staying away from a glass of wine that you know, you just know, would fix everything, cure the headache and cure the craziness and cure the sorrys, the anxiety and uncertainty and cure the uselessness. With certainty, a glass of pinot noir would fix everything, would unclench these jaws. Have I told you that Z bought me a new wine? A velvety-smooth, black pinot noir wine.

He's quieted down. But I want to get up from behind this desk and open the door from this room where I write, walk the hall to the kitchen for a refresh of coffee. Surely my appearance will stoke his hope that he will be fed. Will he stay quieted down? Honestly, he's so fat anyhow. He got fat after our seventeen-year-old Boots died, our mean-girl Boots, another stray I picked up along the way. Mine has been a life of revolving doors and continuous strays. Friends who know me, who stand by me through my impermanence, friends who know me would attest to the revolving doors of the many homes – what was last count – through which I've brought continuous strays.

Now there was a screamer if there ever was one, little tuxedo-cat Boots. God rest her soul. We buried her under a juniper a year after we moved into this house, in an island created when we hired a guy with a backhoe to carve out a driveway that loops from the dusty road up and around the front of the house and back to the road. It's a pear-shaped driveway, the gravel an aggregate material of cut rocks that does not roll under the tires and does not emit dust like what wafts from the dirt road. It's a long driveway, if you care to know, about two hundred feet from entry to stem of pear and return. It's the loop I walk for the morning paper, afternoon mail, ditto to carry buckets of water to the Charlie-Brown pine trees struggling to survive at road's edge, trees planted by a previous owner, before the drought we are in now. May as well call these trees strays also, so responsible I feel for their survival.

It suddenly occurs to me I may be on my lasts: last strays, last cat, last dog, last man, last house, last revolving door, even last breaths. They are numbered you know, our heartbeats and breaths. We're born with just so many and when we use them up, then it's lights out. Recent medical tests reveal my heart beats extras. Does this mean I'm speeding things up, pushing myself to the edge, preparing for that epic swan dive into the abyss?

We buried Boots under the juniper that grows in the middle of this island, where I greet her every morning when I go out with the dog, buried her with the cremated remains of another stray, Wally. They're together in the same grave, dug deep to keep coyotes from ever sniffing them out, to keep them together forever, as they are in my heart. If I never leave this place where now I live, it may be because I don't want to leave their grave. Until I buried these cats, I did not fully understand the comfort of a grave.

So it must be ironic even to me that for most of my adult life I've advocated for cremation, for when I do exhale that last breath, because I have not wanted to take up space, not wanted to bother anyone with my dying, with the business of dying: obituary, services, cards and flowers, burial attire and a burial box (by the time of my death, I will have shrunk to fit into an under-the-bed storage bin). Besides, where would I do such a thing? Where would I die among people I loved, who loved me? I haven't lived anywhere long enough to want to die *there*, to say, bury me *there*.

I console myself with stories of pioneer women who died on their journey to wherever their men brow-beat them to believe was paradise just over the next horizon, just beyond those mountains and then beyond the horizon beyond the mountains that just appeared when they made it to *there*. I'll never make it to *there*. I'll die from exhaustion passing through so many *theres*, so many revolving doors, caring for so many strays; I'll die from heartbreak from never having found *there*, home, my home, among my people, my *there*. I'll die like a Mormon woman who never made it from Missouri to Utah, her grave marked by a wood cross atop a mound of rocks under which she lay, the ground too frozen to dig, her hopes and dreams melting in the spring thaw to water the white-blooming dogwoods nearby.

I don't want to die here. Not here. Nor will I die in the town where I was born. But I have requested that Z scatter my ashes over my mother's grave, in the church cemetery in the town where she was born, the same town I was born, where she rests next to my father (hardly a rest), down a gentle slope from her mother and father, their sisters and brothers, a few rows from my mother's two sisters, one for which I am named and a few headstones away from an unmarked grave where lies her seventh child, her infant daughter. I can't be buried *there* in that cemetery because the church that owns it reserves what plots remain for the remains of their own. For their own. I belong nowhere where I could be counted as one of their own.

I've been sneaking around the house in the dark and in the silence because I don't want to upset my cat who, resigned he wasn't going to get fed, finally went back to my warm spot in the bed. I'll be quiet, sit in my office and type and turn on the internet to view the overnight news. I need to know if there is a government shutdown this morning. I need to know if my husband, the last of my men strays, will come home early from his assignment because that's what happens when federal employees are away from their posts when the government shuts down; they're ordered to return immediately. Which means I'll have to make a dash for the finish line with my chore list, especially, to clean his bathroom, scrub the toilet and sink and shower and floors, the glass shower doors, the tile around the sink and the tile shower and bathroom floors, polish the faucets, pull up the sink plunger and pull out all those whiskers stuck in soap scum in the drain down there. *There*! Now there's a *there*! Yuk! He has no clue. He would never think to clean anything beyond swiping a towel across a fogged mirror to see to shave.

He can have no understanding for what I went through just to clean the ceiling fan, over our bed, where I had to balance myself with feet apart on the foam mattress like feet apart on a surfboard, arms overhead, and wipe the blades with a sponge of warm water and white vinegar, ditto the motor mechanism, plus getting in there with damp cotton swabs to pull out the dust clusters clinging to the mesh that's supposed to keep the dust out, from gumming up the motor. He would never think to do that. I don't know why I bother. He'll never notice and if he does, he would fail to acknowledge results for deeds done because one must have appreciation for what goes into getting something done.

I ask myself and hear you, gentle reader, ask too, haven't I anything better to do? Sometimes I think I should just die in this house, make a point of it, to die in this house, make a plan of it, lay myself down on a freshly made bed under a freshly cleaned spinning ceiling fan, lay myself down to die, because I'm ready, because my heartbeats are about ready to expire and the autopsy will read I died from boredom, from cleaning, from loneliness, boredom and sadness and not from the drink. I'm too proud to be declared dead due to drink.

If I die now, I can stop cleaning. And me, a purpose-driven woman who believes her existence, her legacy, will be marked on leaving this earth and her house and everything associated with her, in clean, operating, Godliness order, just so that no one has to clean up after her when she's gone!

I darned the socks, but I've yet to finish the upper kitchen cabinets. I finally put the step-stool back in the garage and haven't brought it out again. In and out of the garage with that step-stool intending to rub beeswax oil into the desert dry upper kitchen cabinets, but unanswerably unable to complete the job. What's that all about? I reason that I'll get to those cabinets another day, because he may be coming home sooner than planned and because, really, he'll never notice anyhow.

No wonder I have a headache. I aim to be an extraordinary housewife with an extraordinarily clean house with polished pine cabinets and pristine white china toilets that reflect his face when he stands over the bowl. I want to be and for the most part am an extraordinarily efficient housewife, with a pinot noir under the sink.

I'm so ready to make a run for it today. If there's no government shutdown, if Z isn't sent home, after I drop off the cat for his dental procedures that will keep him at the vet's sedated for the rest of the day, I'm going to make a run for it. I'll leave the dog at home and take my secret money envelope and my life in my hands and anyone else's who's on the road and head out to a casino. If only for an hour. Just for a fix. I need a fix. A fix to settle these nerves and unclench these jaws. A fix to be out and about among the living, walking-dead seniors just like me. It's either a ching-ching or a drink. I'm going out for a spin with intent to win, to feel euphoric for even the minutest of a win. But alas, to lose is to face futility for having tried to escape at all. To lose would mean back to the cell again, behind the bars of loneliness again. To lose at the casino would mean I will definitely need that drink.

February 10

Going Dark
  It's not dark yet, but it's getting there – Bob Dylan, *Not Dark Yet.*

February 11

Dark

February 12

The curtains that hang on either side of the stage of my life open and close with the randomness of *whether;* especially, whether my husband is home. Friends and readers of my musings are aware that I have classified myself for many years as a single married woman. In fact, a university press published a piece I wrote about this. I'm sure I'm not unique in this category. Likely, most women my vintage would understand the duality of this status. Single for our single-mindedness, for our need (and comfort) to be alone, independent and self-realising; married for our concession to a cultural norm, a partnership. The single married status is unique in its regular intervals of singlehood within the marriage.

For days one through nine of this month, while Z was away, I fully engaged and devoted myself to singlehood, except for those minor road spurs categorically belonging to marriage, the same of which theoretically contribute to maximum enjoyment of a single married woman's duality. Theoretically.

So that you know, I never made it to the casino. After taking my cat to the vet for what turned out to be extensive dental work, upon depositing him there for half the day, I turned right around and drove myself safely back to the house. I dared not leave the vicinity just in case. Because once I dropped him off, I immediately began to worry more for his well-being than my own chances for changing my destiny, that is, had I won enough money to do so.

I worried that my ten-year-old cat could die on the table and where would I be but on a fat-ass cushy black stool in front of a Quick-Hits penny slot machine, hoping with all my heart that I could possibly win the $10,000 jackpot that would alter the circumstances of my life from then on and forever. As if a mere $10,000 could do that.

Instead, I thought about my cat's wellness and my responsibility to same. What kind of mother would drop off her child at pre-school and then make haste to a casino? The same kind of mother that would uncork a bottle of pinot noir when she really needed to be *there*, a hundred percent *there*, for her sick and needy cat. Really, I do have some moral fibre, some sense of responsibility for my duties as I have created and assumed them, whether single or married, with or without a sick cat.

And yes, I did stop at the store. On my way to pick up the patient to bring him home I stopped and bought a bottle of pinot noir because, I justified, I would need that drink at the end of the day, when I put on my pointy paper hat of wife again, and when my happiest of happy husbands comes home.

In fact, I had planned on that drink, plotted to have the bottle at the ready, under the sink; after all, I would need that drink, deserved that drink, to prepare myself for the role of wife again. When he returns from these long absences, I gird myself for the role of a dutiful, responsible wife with husband, household, and pet responsibilities. Don't misunderstand, I love my home, husband and pets, but I don't necessarily always love my life, or them in my life. And a bottle of wine under the sink provides salve for that.

Oh, less I forget, this date on February 12, 2000: the anniversary of my mother's death. She always said she would make it to the millennium and indeed, she did. I'm thinking of you, my mother, my friend, looking forward to the day when I meet up with you again, when I reach out for your hand to assist me in my crossover to the other side. Perhaps, when we do meet up again, I can ask the hard questions I never thought to ask until now. Why didn't you make good on all those mornings-after, your assurances to your children that you would finally leave? Why didn't you crack Frank upside the head with a cast iron skillet like you said you would, if even some day? Why didn't you warn me of the side effects of getting old?

February 13

After dark, comes light. So far. With threats of nuclear attacks and extremes in climate change, one day I may wake up in the dark at 4:35 a.m. and it may remain dark. Or one day I may not wake up and for sure, it will be dark.

I went dark over the weekend for two reasons: my husband came home very late Friday night – his presence changes everything – and my brother JJ from upstate New York (yes, the same brother about to lose a leg) called on Saturday afternoon from the Interstate forty minutes away to say he was on his way. On his way? What? From where? To here? But who knew? The first words that tumbled from my mouth: *But I don't have any food in the house!* I was not prepared to play hostess to a houseguest, regardless of relation.

Z slept in till noon Saturday and by the time he got himself up and going, it was too late to go to town, or more accurately, Hoke did not feel like driving his Miss Daisy to get groceries. He was tired from his long week on the road and I, well, it's beyond me now with my glaucoma to get in the car and drive myself to town. Like the moon Titania circling Uranus, my life and all its doings revolve around Z. With the onslaught of glaucoma, getting older (these are stages, too, both of them, stages in life, as well as stages I must step out on regardless of fright), ahem, nothing is like it used to be, however that was, because besides failing eyesight, I struggle to contend with failing memory. Have I mentioned this before? These days I don't try to remember. I let the memories lapse like bubbles that break before they fly from the wand out of the bubble bottle. But I do wish my few and far between neighbours understood better that I can't just up and grab the keys and get in the car and go. Meaning, they know Z is away a lot; they know I could use some help getting to town. Then again, maybe they don't know. Maybe I'm that insignificant to them. Wish I wasn't so alone. So much alone.

By the time my brother JJ arrived, we had picked up beer and pizza from the joint next to the gas station across the highway, and I had readied the guestroom and pulled all my personals from the second bathroom for his private use. At the kitchen table we caught up on scant news. Really, we could not recount the last time we saw each other but left it at the occasion fifteen years back when Z and I drove from where we lived then, in a six-hundred-fifty-foot cabin perched on a mountainside of the Western Sierras, when we drove to north central California to attend JJ's son's funeral, his only child, a funeral for a young man who allegedly walked in front of a moving train.

After about ninety minutes and more nice-nice small talk we all went to bed. I got up early to make breakfast and help JJ out the door. I'm guessing he could be nearing our sister HH's place in northeast Ohio (yes, the sister to whom I promised a kidney), near our hometown, where we six were all born, where our mother was born and our parents are buried, where their parents are buried, where number seven is buried, along with generations of aunts, uncles, cousins on either side of the family, childhood friends and neighbours and simple hometown folk. My home. I really do have a home; that graveyard, in that town, a place I could theoretically call home; that hometown with that parish cemetery. But I never admit to it, that I have a home, where all these relations are buried. Last time I visited HH and we went to the cemetery to say hello, to have a family reunion of sorts, among the dead, I made an inquiry at the parish office to buy a plot but the church to which I once belonged said no, but I've already shared this with you, that their precious plots are reserved for current members of the parish. So maybe I don't have a home. Maybe I was destined from birth to never have a home.

The men drank beer with the pizza and you guessed it, I poured myself a glass of pinot noir. I don't know exactly when that bottle was opened, but it was there, corked and almost full, waiting patiently, my pinot noir, under the sink, opened and waiting for me. Let's see, today is Tuesday. I finished that bottle yesterday, late Monday afternoon, while I sat on the sofa with my knitting, tuned in to the Winter Olympics, waiting for Z to come home. It was dark; the dog and cat were in; Z's dinner was ready, ready to be set at the table where he eats and reads the newspaper, as I rarely eat that late, or more often than not, I just don't eat. But I was sipping the last dregs from that bottle of wine, content on the couch, having happy hour alone, ready and waiting for my husband to come home.

I'd have to look back through the pages to see how long a stretch I made it between drinks. Four, maybe five days? Probably fewer. Nonetheless, I'm set to start all over again. I'll try to go the day without a drink and try to restart my goal again, to make it through these remaining days of the month without a drink.

A new word popped up from a page: *pedant*. There was a time in my life when I knew what it meant and I could offer a good guess right now, but I'm so unsure of my shrinking vocabulary and shrinking capacity to remember that I'd rather not embarrass myself by taking a chance. Worse, what can happen, I'll look it up and repeat aloud the meaning many times over hoping to commit it to memory but by tomorrow I will not remember *pedant*. And I'll find no use for trying to use it in conversation because it's likely I may speak to no one, except the dog and cat and as they have done when I've tried this, they'll just look up at me quizzically as if to ask if that's something for them to eat. Perhaps I've shared this obsession with unreliable memory with you before.

Maybe now's a good time to interject my thoughts on flaws. I mentioned David Brooks writing about people who led such lives of notable moral character, one need not wonder why they became the role models and mentors and leaders and proven principled people that they were. He sets them up on pedestals for his readers to admire and then, graciously, he topples them with a quick chop to their loosely attached marble heads for us to watch roll. He exposes their flaws. And they all have them. We all have them. Oh, how I love the flaw, as much as I love the drink.

February 14

February 14, Valentine's Day. The pressure is on. A commercial occasion pushed by florists and candy and card makers and lingerie sellers to remind us that we must spend, buy, buy, buy, in order to prove our love. Money does indeed equate to love.

I would not have remembered it had it not been for going into the corner store yesterday to buy eggs. I'd used them all up on my brother's visit and I needed to boil eggs for my husband's salad. So into the store I go and right there at the entrance – I had to be careful not to knock over the display which I'm apt to bump into just as I am with other shoppers and their carts I sadly cannot see – right there for me to bump into are gleaming glass vases of love: long-stemmed red-bud roses.

It never occurred to me until I went into my bathroom at four this morning, when not the first time, but on the next go-round, when I went back to put drops in my eyes, did I notice the vase with a single red rose and a stem of baby's breath, still wrapped in its cellophane, set at the edge of the sink, to the left, where I was careful not to knock over my husband's display of affection for me. I suppose now I will have to display mine for him: *Oh, thank you. Thank you*! Hurry, hurry, kiss, kiss. *Happy Valentine's Day honey, I love you, too*, before he runs out the door to catch the 6:08.

It's hours later and, of course, my train of thought has gone choo-choo down the tracks of lost memory and I will have to try to gain momentum again. Forget about picking up where I left off. There's no such thing, you know, our thoughts are not like shiny dimes dropped on the floor, easy to pick out and pick up. Even when I play word association games, or go through the entire English alphabet three times hoping that when I light on a letter a word will jar loose and aha! I'll remember what it was I was going to do. With diminishing capacity to see, diminishing capacity to remember; it's truly out of sight out of mind for me.

What I had wanted to remember, what came to me when my mind went blank, magically re-entered stage right. It's magic I rely on, abracadabra! Poof! A memory like a rabbit pulled from a top hat suddenly appears.

Have you ever gone out the door with genuine intent to be somewhere for a specific reason only to find yourself *there* but with no desire to continue in the endeavour? That happened to me yesterday. I collected my knitting project – yes, another woollen winter hat – yarn, needles, tape measure, tiny scissors, all the supplies I need fit in a vintage yellow Tupperware bowl – grabbed my tiny purse, key ring with two keys, leashed my dog and went out the front door of this tiny house with plenty of time to arrive at the large and lovely living room in the old but renovated railroad depot community building, probably less than three miles away, around the bend past the elementary school, four stop signs and four turns, a right, a left, a right, a left, from where I live now. I say now, because one day last week, I looked out the window over my shoulder where I write and I could swear I was somewhere else, in another house, in the room where I wrote when I lived there, where I could look out the window over my shoulder and see my neighbour's house and yard with a very big and sprawling-limbed tree. Only now I can't remember if it was an oak or an elm or a sycamore, or none of the above, only that it was big and beautiful and that I loved looking at that tree. Here, where I live now, I look out the window to my right and what do I see but a cholla, a stumpy, prickly sprawling-limbed, not-so-pretty, threatening and did I say prickly? Cholla. It's not even green, not a pure forest green, but more of a pukey, hangover green. Alas, won't be long and I'll be embracing that cholla, not literally, but appreciating it nonetheless for what it is, for its ability to thrive, exactly where it is. Would I could be so blessed.

As I was saying, yesterday, I got to where I was going for this aforementioned somewhere, the living room of the community building, ten minutes early and the reason I was early because generally, I am always early. When I arrived at the depot, where I generally arrive ten minutes early, I went to an adjacent building to say hello to the homeowners' association covenant compliance coordinator – cute little man who, when he refers to recently observed women, he positions both hands cupped at his chest and describes these women wholly in terms of the size of their breasts. Whether he spots these women's yum-yums in church or at a committee meeting or the corner store, he zeroes in on that part of their anatomy. I speculate that it's because he's short and his eyes have nowhere else to go but to zero in on their breasts. B-o-i-i-n-g!

I'm not sure why I've made a point of visiting with this little man for the better part of the two years I've been going to knitting, but on every Tuesday before knitting, I take my dog and we visit with him for just those few minutes. What we have in common is that he's from a town in Vermont where I attended graduate school; basically, we discovered that we once roamed the same campus, albeit years apart as he is much younger and now we share nostalgia for a once-upon-a-time, feel-good and fondly-remembered experience.

But yesterday, due to a schedule change for the finance committee meeting, he was not in his office. He was out. And because he was out and not in, well, this changed the course of action I had originally laid out for my day and I thereupon, on the spot, decided to nix the knitting.

With extra time on my side for his not being in, I decided to skip knitting. I did not want to go to the living room of the adjacent building, the depot, ten minutes early, so I turned away from the little man's locked door, walked back to the car and drove off with my yellow Tupperware bowl and dog to the corner store to buy that carton of eggs.

Never in my dreams, whether wild or tame, had I ever envisioned myself attending knitting meetings with a group of later middle-aged women. Don't get me wrong, these are congenial, respectable, engaging women (yes, you question, what is a not-so congenial, disrespectable, disengaging woman like me doing, supplanting herself like pigweed in a pansy patch), anywhere from eight to eighteen who show up like loyal AAs for their group gathering every Tuesday, to share their progress with their projects – some stitches and patterns so challenging I would not dare to attempt, mostly because I can't see the point. Get it? Can't see the point! They gather to share their interests in spinning wool from the alpacas they raise on the ranches they own and also to share their interests in spinning yarns of sweetness and continuity and belonging that goes on in their lives; where they once lived (Atlanta, Boston, Chicago, Cleveland, Dallas, Denver, sophisticated places, unlike my last home in Pocatello), before they moved here; where they once worked, in careers where they proved themselves contenders, among colleagues and friends and families they still stay in contact with (I sense myself the lone drifter), the same which come to stay in their casitas (and I don't mean the little white bubble trailer hitched behind a half-ton pickup rolling along an interstate enroute to a campground), all us knitters in this group, in this renowned world-class, resort destination. Do you know what a destination is? It's the end.

These lovely women, these civic-minded women who eagerly put roots down, invest themselves in the guilds and charities of this community, these talented knitters, they gracefully refrain from gossip, politics, even age-related conditions, like arthritis, cancer, hair loss, glaucoma. In this, they are more gracious than I have ever been or will be. I'm not one to keep a complaint to myself. Yes, I've made them aware of my glaucoma, for which I received the sympathy I sought, but not an understanding for what the condition is. Yet in this moment of weakness, admitting to my disability did not unburden me, did not ease the disgruntlement, the unfairness I feel for my life's lot by any measure. Obviously, they are women of substance, while I could be referred to as a woman of substance abuse. They bear up well; carry themselves erect and proud, like dowager mistresses over their desert oasis manors.

As a collective, we are all survivors – we've made it thus far. We sit in that community room and work our needles and yarn, click, click, clickety-click. A few struggle with gnarled knuckles without a mention of discomfort. In fact, three have left the group for another destination, for a walk on over to the other side, never to return again. That's about as brow-raising as it gets in that klatch.

Remind me if I've already shared this. Or don't. But if I've already shared this, I may be telling it to you again, yes, but certainly not in the same way, because I could never remember enough of what I said in the first place to say it again the same way. Nevertheless, you are free to skip down to the next paragraph, or just throw this yarn (story, not material, although yarn is material, but not for books, for woollen hats and I wouldn't suggest you throw the hat away, there might be a rabbit under it) but I would understand if you throw this book away entirely. I would understand.

While JJ was here, the minutes before we said goodbye, in those few minutes, maybe two, I said: *Well, I don't know if I'll ever see you again, but just so you know, because I want to tell you this, if I go between now and then, Z will have everything taken care of. There will be no services. He'll cremate me and sprinkle my ashes over Mum's grave*, in that cemetery where they won't let me in as a whole corpse, because I no longer belong to that parish. I'll fly like dust in the wind over the mounds and humps of clay, come to rest upon the sunken hallow ground under which in various spots lay mother, father, sister, grandparents, aunts, uncles, neighbours, friends; I'll float into nooks and crannies of weather-worn headstones, stone-carved and cold, angels with broken wings. Home. Finally, home. Rest. Finally rest. No, I didn't say all that, but when I hugged him goodbye at his open car door, for real, I said: *See you, Bro, on the other side.*

Mine is a small world, after all. And it shrinks further with each passing day. I shrink too. Z says to me: *You're so little. How did you ever get so little? It's the law*, I said, *of diminishing returns.* We're supposed to get more little, so as not to take up so much space in the end. It's our destiny, to get little, to shrink and get little and blow like dust in the wind in the end.

I've made a point of getting smaller as I age, of taking up less space. I don't need much space anymore, don't need much of anything anymore. Just room enough for Minnie me and my under-the-sink, at the ready, bottle of pinot noir.

February 15

An overnight snow. Lovely, like the women in the knitting circle, calm, accepting for their place at this time of their lives, accepting as the snow is of this season. I could learn something from this snow, to every season, turn; and those women, to every birthday, turn. At least from what they convey during these short two hours, one day a week, but what can I know of their pasts, their troubles, heartaches and loss? What do I know except what they bring in that day, beautifully created cable-knit sweaters, knit-in-the-round hats and gloves; their own designs and their own wool spun from their own alpacas, yarn richly dyed in colours of the season too.

But I'm not a late bloomer, late-in-lifer who still yearns to learn: how to raise and shear sheep or alpacas; how to gather and spin their wool; how to select the perfect native flower blooms for their texture and colour, to dry and dye the wool. I shot my wad years ago and now I'm spent. In fact, it occurred to me last evening that I might be good for this side of a decade, in mind and body, if I'm lucky and so blessed and if that's the case, if that thought about being good for this side of a decade, if that is God putting me on notice, then I'd be wise to wake up and start to have fun.

If I'm to learn anything, then I want to learn how to have late-in-life fun. I want to get out and do it. Just do it, especially because of my glaucoma. I'm not interested in AARP's panel-prescribed suggestions for senior fun, which I have no idea for what they suggest, because I hardly read the magazine, way too upbeat for me, would hardly heed, because, in my opinion, I'm not their target audience. Come to think of it, why do I subscribe?

I want my own; my own compounded prescription for fun; my own sense for glee; I want to get out and find my own. I want to speak my own. I want to laugh uproariously, to put a hand on my belly because it aches, to catch my breath because I'm about to faint from too much fun; I want to feel dropper-size tears roll down and over the moguls of my wrinkled face. I want to get out of myself and my self-imposed exile. I want to live!

Such bravado! I'm good. It's all good. Put down the gothic novel. Now back to real life.

Yesterday, Valentine's Day and also Ash Wednesday. Almost forgot that along with Valentine's Day this year, came Ash Wednesday. *Dust thou art and dust thou shalt return.* That wispy stuff I mop from the shelves when it gets thick and grey, when I can finally see that it's *there*. My husband never sees it, never sees the dust on the shelves, the clusters of pet hair that roll against the baseboards, the pink ring around the toilet bowl. Me, I have to get up close and personal to see just about anything these days, stick my head in the bowl sometimes, my gloved hand gripping a pumice stone. I try to explain to him my visual limitations, like the eleven and two o'clock tunnel I peer through, the tunnel that gets narrower and blacker on the sides; I try to explain to him how one-dimensional it all appears to me, like when I step off a curb. He tries to understand, I think. I would like to think.

I want to talk about influence, under the influence, the influence of sick adults on innocent children, the influence of violence widely depicted in video games and movies, played out on the streets and in schools; the influence of drugs and alcohol, these examples of how to conduct a life. What does that mean, to be under the influence? Is it the same as under a spell?

After I enjoy a bowl of Cheerios with ripened blackberries floating over whole milk, am I then under the influence of lacto fatty acids that could affect how I behave? Behave. Who wants to behave? What of an early afternoon indulgence in two quarts of buttered salted popcorn? Am I then under the influence of an overdose of carbs? A goblet of pinot noir influences my behaviour, but it's the thoughts running through my head that cause me to reach for that bottle from under the sink in the first place.

Dust thou art. Compost thou art. I understand bodies can now be composted at licensed facilities, bagged and toted home to use as fertiliser for the tomatoes. I don't know if I'm there yet, agreeable to composting, but it's a practical and likely cost-effective method of dealing with remains. As I may have mentioned earlier, as things stand today, I've requested that Z cremate me and sprinkle my ashes over my mother's grave; more specifically, that he do so on a calm rainy day, when rain can secure me and no wind can blow a speck of me over to the side of Frank.

Almost seventy years old and I still walk in the shadow of Frank. Under the influence of Frank. My biological father and male parent Frank. Unschooled, street-smart, Lithuanian immigrant. World War II, thirteen-medal-awarded hero. A behind-the-velvet-curtain Oz, card room gambler and drunk. Bar-room brawler, wife-beater, baby killer. A drunk, a son of a drunk. A little man with a heavy hand and a heavy influence on me. I suffer under his spell, his yeasty beer and stale Lucky Strike smell and reach for the drink.

February 16

Instead of two sheets to the wind, I am two days to the good! So I've got a new start date, February 14. Valentine's Day and the start of Lent. If I can make it through the end of this month, then I just may call it good, fourteen days good; then again, if I can make it through the end of the month, I just may go the distance, all the way through Lent, forty days to Easter. Wouldn't that be something? Yes, indeed. That would be something.

Imagine who I might become! *Me*! I'm imagining *me*! I'm imagining who/what I could become: happy? (sometimes I think I am happy, but maybe I could get more happy without the drink); healthy? (while I appear healthy enough, I can't possibly know the toll of the drink on my overall health, the health of my organs, that kidney I promised HH, to say nothing of the health of my brain). Then again, I buy into the science that extols the heart health benefits of the red-wine drink.

Still, it is a virtue, is it not, to abstain from the drink? The virtuous know it because they do it, all the time. But that's because it's written in the covenants of God, in the twelve steps of AA, in the Book of Mormon, in the Quran (2:219): *They ask you about wine and gambling. Say, in them is great sin and [yet, some] benefit for people. But their sin is greater than their benefit.* Should I abstain, I could actually become virtuous. But really, why would I want to do that?

No, I won't go for gold, I mean, perpetual sobriety. Can't see the point. I'll be content enough to have competed with myself in this one rather Olympic feat: to abstain from drink for a reasonable amount of time if just to learn who I really am, without the drink. And who knows, I may be nobody, the same as who I am with the drink, a nobody, nobody really different, no different at all from the woman who enjoys her sip-sip of pinot noir, the drink from the bottle under the sink.

Richard Rohr writes about seeking *daily bread* to feed the starving soul; fresh and *living water* to fill our reservoir. *Authentic recovery is not actually about mere sobriety as much as it is about simple and ever-deeper connection with what is. Deep connection is our goal and it frees us from all loneliness, separateness and boredom, as is far beyond just stopping the addiction behaviour.* While Rohr is thinking spirituality, I am thinking wine. I can connect pretty deeply with my pinot noir. For now, that seems to be my food for the starving soul, my living water, my spiritual connection with *what is.*

Let me digress on this *what is.* The first time I heard an acquaintance of mine say, *it is what it is,* I just about slugged the guy. That's woo-woo talk, I thought to myself, double-speak coming from a man who just wanted to shrug off something important to me, something I wanted him to see as relevant to me. How dare him; how dare he dismiss me with a sling of *what is.*

Lately, however, I accept just about everything as a *what is.* I feel so powerless to change anything from *what is* to what

I would like it to be. While I don't feel powerless to put down the drink, uh, that's set it down on the table, not chug it, I do feel genetically wired to drink and that philosophically, it's what I'm going to give myself permission to do. I knowingly understand and accept the *what is* and *why it is*, that I drink. Accepting doesn't mean I have to change, however, and that's a relief that I don't have to change. But I do have to be watchful, to live with *what is* and all its consequences. Call me a late-bloomer in this one thing: learning to live with my genes, learning to live forgivingly with Frank in my genes, learning to live respectfully with the drink in my genes. Better to learn from and understand than to put it upon myself to give it up.

In sorting through boxes while Z is away and out of the way, one day last week, I pulled a carton off a shelf in the garage to give it a look-see. It's my goal to rid myself of possessions which possess me.

Into the box I crawled, like a cockroach inside a dark cupboard, hungry to stumble onto a find, or better, something of which I could de-possess.

I've been a thrift store junkie for as long as I can remember, caught up in the thrill of the find. But I avoid those stores now. Scavenging through a Goodwill, Habitat re-sale warehouse, St. Vincent de Paul Thrift – the list is long – foments in my genes, this on my mother's side, from her father, a Polish immigrant and refugee. He had numbers tattooed on his arm, or were they inked on the inside of his wrist? but I never knew, or asked, what for. A junk collector, he roamed the alleys behind his house in the old lumber mill and manufacturing part of town, combing the railroad tracks, picking up treasures if you will. He filled a falling-down dirt-floor shed in the back of his house, my mother's birthplace, with a junk-collector's treasure trove of copper, brass, nails, depression-era glass, finders-keepers kinds of junk. When he died, my grandmother called another junkie to haul it all away.

I drift. Inside that carton I pulled from the shelf in my garage, I found a journal, actually a stash of clothbound books, yellowed and water damaged, but decipherable nonetheless. Selecting none in particular, I skimmed the pages until I came upon an entry I wanted to read further. At first, I could not place the story of what it was I felt compelled then to put to page. Like a time traveller trying to affix herself to a floating milepost in space, when I paused long enough to think, I began to remember.

One Sunday morning, I decided to retrieve the journal and read that passage to Z. He was sitting up in bed with his coffee and newspaper. Allowing me his attention, I opened the journal to November 11, 1990; bear with me as I share with you:

I push a wheelchair up against Adam's urine bag to hide it from view. Then I pull a curtain to hide Clifford's handless limbs waving in mid-air, but not before he kicks off his sheet revealing he wears no bottoms.

Adam begins to chant. No words, only a rhythmic monotone of ya ya ya ya ya ya ya. He begs for my hand with his eyes and an outstretched arm. He just wants to touch me, hold onto my hand. He puts my hand against his lips and kisses it, like an old-school gentleman greeting a lady for the first time. Gently, I try to pull my hand away and he just as gently persists in holding it. I look into his eyes and see his despair. I know I am stronger so I pull my hand away. Ya ya ya ya ya ya ya.

I secretly wish that he would be so heartbroken by my rejection that he would die. Right there. In front of me. He would ya ya no more.

Drapes over the single window in the room block out most of the afternoon light. Parting them just a crack so I can see enough to write in my journal, I bring a second wheelchair to my father's bed, brush off the crumbs on the sheepskin cover before I sit. He may not know I am here. He lies with his face to the wall. It's too painful for him to sit up, in a bed or a chair. He hurts all over.

I'm leaving tomorrow and I just want to sit with him alone. Alone with my father, Frank. Now there's a scary thought. I really don't have anything to say and there is nothing I want to hear him say. I feel nothing for him – not anger, not love, nor pity. I feel only the necessity for my own experience. I feel a need to awaken, to thaw from years of frozen fear and contempt.

My father calls me by my name and I get up from the chair to stand by his side. He is so frail, lying there like a small sick child, bed rails up and locked to keep him inside and safe. It is hard to imagine him the mean bully he was, for the entire span of my eighteen years of living under his rule, the mean bully he once was who could thump chests and lash backs with his thick leather belt, drag his daughters by their ponytails across a room and twist his sons' ears to disfigurement.

A headache is coming on; the tension of holding back tears is getting too tight for me. I refuse to cry. I refuse to lose my tolerance for being with my father, with these men, their drooling, their vacant eyes, their smell, their ya ya ya ya ya ya ya, their toothless faces and open sores, their grabbing to hold onto me.

Tomorrow I leave. I will leave my mother to visit her husband, my father, in this nursing home day after day, to complain that his pyjamas are missing, the floor is dirty, his bed needs changing, the bill is too high. Tomorrow I return to California where the sun shines, while the gloomy days of winter settle in here. Tomorrow I will put behind my mother's pleas for me to stay, the boarded-up buildings on Main Street and the inevitable doom, the pungency of dying; I'll put aside recollection for ever having been in this nursing home, next to my father's bed. But I won't forget his helplessness; finally, blessedly, it has come. He can't hurt me anymore, but I know better. He will haunt me just as whatever demons haunt him. And I'll learn to live with that. Somehow, I will.

Clifford moans loudly now. I'm afraid to look at him but I do. He touches his knee with the stub of his arm, his leg and arm both thin as matchsticks.

Adam is quiet.

My father stops aching aloud. He knows I'm here. Will he know I am gone tomorrow? Will he miss me when I am gone? I cannot stop the tears.

He has soiled himself terribly and there is blood everywhere, on his backside, on the hospital-white sheets. He cries out in pain. He wants something for his pain. I go to the nurses' station and ask for help. An orderly brings a mashed aspirin and shoves it into my father's mouth with a popsicle stick. No water. Dad is hating it. He hates the bitter taste of the mashed pill. I beg him to swallow the medicine. Please, Dad, it will help with the pain. Would that a mashed pill could help me with my pain, too. The orderly leaves.

My father spits out the vile white stuff in a paper towel I hold under his chin. He refuses water. He turns over in his misery to the wall. And I wipe the tears from my eyes with the back of my hand. I too am miserable, so miserable I must leave.

I hesitate to kiss him on his cheek to say goodbye as I really don't want to go. I don't want to go out into the hallway looking like this, my face flushed, tears running down and dropping so fast I can't shore them up. I don't want anyone out there to see my sorrow. They may think I'm crying for my father, but I'm really crying for me, my suffering, my grief, my loss, me.

February 17

Maybe thirty years ago, I read a book whose title and subject matter was about honouring the god in everything, something Rohr more recently calls panentheism. I'm not a student of world religion – certainly no longer a new-ager – but believing in that spark of divine helps me wake up in the morning and soldier through the day, especially after a no-rest night, a non-restorative fretful fitful night. Last night's sleep wasn't any worse or better than any other, except for a strange dream about a big two-storey white weathered clapboard farmhouse that sat tall and spooky at the end of a paved road, just before a dirt one beyond meandered on. Nothing in the dream indicated where that house was, probably in some small town I could have lived in or visited, but regardless, it was for sale and I wanted to buy it, which makes no sense because I have no desire to be responsible for a big old house that needs painting and a big piece of property that needs tending. It's just now occurring to me that maybe I wanted to buy that house because it needed me. Anything can happen in a dream, especially the preposterous.

For some, it may seem preposterous to think, or imagine, that God inhabits everything. Rohr writes about this and he also writes that nature is the first Bible. *The first act of divine revelation is creation itself. Thus, nature is the first Bible.*

I like to practise what I read, like to take suggestions for something to think about, to chew on; sometimes I try them on like new pieces of clothing and wear them for a day or so. Some become a part of me, like the projection of the divine onto everything, whether a rock or blade of grass or worm or one of those thorny goat heads that stick to my socks, get inside my shoes, attach to the tender pads of my dog's paws when we go through brush on our walks. Actually, it's easy to see God in my dog. Look, they're the same three letters that spell out their names. God looks at me through my dog's eyes, those deep dark silky brown eyes that swallowed me whole into the mystery behind them when I first saw her on the reservation land, emaciated, a bow of ribs arching over her abdomen like a dead bloated cow on its side, where I had to step over her to get to the building where I worked, where she lay dying. God made me make her mine. My sweet, sweet brown-eyed girl. It's been six years since I brought her home, to that tall white two-storey house I lived in at the time. Hmm. Not so unlike the house in my dreams, except the one I had in real life was grand, in no need of paint, on an impeccably landscaped property I had so joyously tended, in that house where I so joyously once lived. Unremarkably, it's only in hindsight that I recall joy.

When I take my dog out for her morning walks, that special quiet and private time together helps me to greet the world. I give shoutouts to ravens and bluebirds, passing clouds and giant sacatons, to the rocks atop the site where we buried Boots, beloved Boots, to the twisted chollas and the bunny scurrying out from under the wolfberry. Better run, run bunny run, less a coyote catches you.

Out on the dirt road, I look beyond the brown – everything is brown, varying shades of brown – I look up and over flat-roofed pueblo-brown houses, let my eyes settle on the mountain ranges all around; some under foggy morning sky, others white with snow, still others seemingly within reach, close enough to touch with my gloved hand. On those early mornings when the sun decides to join us, when she throws out her rays like leggy yo-yo strings, she casts golden glows among the peaks and shadows. Then there's the Galisteo Wave: an over-yonder range that on a clear day looks like a towering heave of ocean about to crash to shore.

My God gets a capital G, because my early education in a Catholic school taught me that certain words are, out of respect and for their importance, their sacredness, because who/what they represent demands respect, because in school God always got a big G. And why in this increasingly secular world, why change now? I mean, from a big to a small g. Matters to no one but me and it's important to pay attention to what matters to me; otherwise, what is there to live for, if nothing but for what matters to Me. Capital M for Me. In truth, I rarely make anything be about me. Never learned how.

Late yesterday afternoon a friend called, upset, because I had written her a brief note on my preparedness to depart this world, on how I was making peace with my world. She said: *Now what do you mean you've made peace with me?* I said: *Well maybe it's really that YOU made peace with ME, when you contacted me after decades of absence and made peace with me.*

It's heart-warming to connect with friends with whom you've spent a select section of your life. This friend and I bicycled the beach almost every day, meeting before sunrise to circle a route that had us speed-pedalling home as the blue-black sky turned to purple to orange to yellow to a new golden, surprise-on-the-horizon kind of day, when we quickly said our goodbyes to return to our respective homes to dress for work, still early, invigorated for our ride with the waking flapping pelicans and screeching seagulls and scruffy-bearded fishermen preparing their boats for their hauls that day.

I'm glad she did, find me, call me, renew our friendship. I'm pretty much squared away with everything, people, places, even tall and spooky white houses. JJ's visit helped me square things away with him and I'm square with my sister HH. It's a good feeling, to be square, to take stock and declare: *so it is; it is what it is.*

I couldn't make my friend comfortable with our conversation, but that was not up to me. If I recollect correctly, she doesn't believe in any God, big or little g, let alone a God in my dog, or even in me. I think she belongs to that group of people who was brought up with a God in their house but who decided they didn't need one anymore and eventually parted ways. I've never parted from my God and to have learned to find God in everything, well, that makes a heaven on earth for me.

Are you sick of me yet? I'm sick of myself, too. What comes with a good (enough) sleep is that it takes the edge off, paves the way for a possibly remarkable day, instead of a feeling of dread, instead of fogginess in the head. Last night's, a testimony to the dream, was a good enough sleep. Yes, I made it through another day without the drink.

February 18

Oh misery! Oh miserable me! Oh sleepless me! Whatever made me think I had come to peace with anything, let alone me? I could've addressed this present misery just after midnight, when I woke up from a miserable sleep with a miserable dream about a beaded rug that the bar owner – because I had admired it while it lay over steps that drunks walked over to pass through the front saloon doors – said I could get it cheap. One of her girls had made it but would sell it cheap because the young woman needed the money. The bar owner asked me: *You want it? I'm sure she'll sell it cheap because she needs the money to pay her debts.* Yes, I wanted that beautifully beaded rug and would have offered to buy it but whomever I was with was already out the door. Four of us had come inside to get something to eat, not drink, just eat. They had already left through the front saloon doors when I was coming up after them and tripped on that rug and they were already out, not waiting in a car, but in a buckboard, because the dream took place way back ago, in the days of the old west.

An outcome of sleeplessness, despite a two-minute dream, is sheer misery for having to get up and take on the day. Actually, a dream like the one above only adds to my misery because it makes no sense, cannot be applied to solving any of the mysteries of my life. And it makes no difference the drink – funny I abstained from the drink in that dream – because I left the bottle under the sink, opened earlier by Z because he needed the drink to do taxes, but I left it alone so I could say to you today: *I made it through another night and day without the drink.* But oh misery! Perhaps I should not be so wilful as to not have the drink. Perhaps I'm a person for the better when I do take that drink.

Z got so miserable working on our taxes yesterday that I got miserable too. Contagious as the flu. He claimed he was going to just kill himself over these goddammed taxes but I said, *No, let me go first, I want to go first. I'm older. It's only right I go first. Let me kill myself first.* Because sometimes living with him is as close to dying as I can get.

Death and taxes. Nothing's for certain except death and taxes; nothing worse than a slow death. A swill from the bottle would be a sure cure, do me fine for now.

I've got to pause and go get the cat. He's outside and a sitting duck for a coyote or bobcat and if I don't be careful, it will be our cat whose death is certain and that would make for more misery and I would never be able to forgive myself if I lose the cat that way and certainly not so soon after we've shelled out hundreds to get his teeth fixed, put out seven hundred dollars for this and our return on investment has yet to be realised. Besides, I love the little guy. I don't want to lose my cat through my own stupid lack of mindfulness, because I was unmindful that he was outside too dark to be and a sitting duck for death.

He's in. Much too dark this early morning for the cat to be out; much too dark and too early for me to be up and about but I'm much too miserable for anything to be any other way than as it is. It's starting out to be an *It is what it is* kind of day.

Z's determined to finish our taxes today. It's a job he hates but won't have any other way. He's in charge and I'm his minion and I let it be that way because it's easy and because it's how it works in this family of four: he, me, dog, cat. I get everything ready for him to enter into the computer. Therein lies an interruption to my otherwise cadenced day: he has to use mine, my old reliable desktop that sits on an old table slightly swayback in the middle, the table next to the window in a tiny room in the back of this tiny house where I often seclude myself, sequestered, secluded, alone with me. I shut the door to the cat because otherwise, he'd hop on the desk and walk across the keyboard to get to the window and who knows what free-verse, gobbly-gook you would have to read through then, what kind of mess the cat could make of our taxes.

But it's my haven, in this house we share, no, my hideout, where I can creep quietly in, in the wee dark hours of the morning, close the door, back in this tiny room where I can sit and be with me, alone with miserable me.

I give it up, my computer and my room, my own private Idaho – no that's not now where I live, but was at one time – I give it up at tax time for Z to sit on my favourite chair (a parting gift from a university where once I taught) and brood. I give this room and chair over to him for his turn at being miserable, too. Maybe misery lives in this room. Beware! Misery lies beyond the door to this room! If I should kill myself, I should do it in this room, put a shotgun between my legs, wedge the barrel under my chin and boom! What a friend of mine did. But I won't. I have no desire to do the deed by pulling my own trigger. Besides, Z calculates a handsome refund and half is mine, in theory. Not that I'll get half because we'll use the money for something like paying off a credit card that we loaded up to fix the cat and fix the car. Did I tell you about the car?

I was without my car (it's not really my car, nothing's really mine, only my misery is mine. It's ours, mine to drive now and then; in truth, it's the dog's). I've been without the car because it was in the shop for major repairs, age-related repairs: battery, brakes, transmission, worn out parts. Would that I could go to a shop for my own age-related repairs! It's fifteen years old and it's what I drive but not very often with this glaucoma, because of which I hardly leave the house anymore. For the car to be in the shop for three and a half days meant no inconvenience to me, meant nothing except an empty space in its parking place next to the fence and forward of a well-established good-size piñon tree where a coyote could hide and surprise my cat and me and that could prove a miserable surprise indeed! Under that tree live creatures, whether rats or gophers or prairie dogs or snakes or vermin of any sort; under that tree are holes and tunnels for a myriad of critters to live and hide and for my cat to pretend he's skulking them from his side, a safe side, to a debatable degree, behind a high wire fence.

I would've liked to have had that rug.

February 19

Well finally, some *zzzzz*s. Sleep came between one and four in the morning. Awake before one because Z woke me with his complaint that he was hot. I must've just rolled over to ignore him but not before I asked the time. *It's one*, he said.

When I woke again, I was pulling his sweatshirt from where he had stuffed it between us. I remember pulling it through the covers like a towel stuck in my mother's old wringer washer – it just kept coming and coming – until I had pulled it all out, bunched it up and flung it across the room. That was about four. I'm still sleeping, mind you, I'm quite sure I did none of this awake, because I was operating inside a bubble of a dream: a repeat dream many times over, a singular dream that when it comes, I finally get a good sleep.

It's a dream about a man I once knew from a long time ago, the same man who introduced me to the line of *It is what it is*. In this dream, we are always about to be married, or separated, or divorcing, or we are divorced and he's moved on to another woman, but he's torn between her and me. He invariably goes back to her – *her* is not always the same other woman. I put up somewhat of a fight, to win him back, but I never do. There was such a man in my earlier years, with whom I fell irretrievably in love, head over heels in love. He broke my heart. I don't know why we keep meeting like this but when we do, I sleep like a woman in love.

Last night we met in an old garden, me and the above man in my dream. Could've been a field, fallow and untended from the harvest the season before. We stood among dry corn stalks bent at their waists to face the ground, their once silky tassels dirty yellow and brittle as straw. These rows of stalks looked like old women frozen in time with their heads bowed in weeping.

This man and me, we looked over the garden space and talked, then argued, about which part of that space I was allowed to plant in the coming spring. We clearly did not agree on where and how much of this space would be allotted to me.

Then next thing I knew the cat had fallen over my side of the bed to the floor – thump! I must have moved suddenly, knocking him to the floor, with his back claws dug into the top sheet. The sound of the claws gripping the sheet woke me from the dream. Mind you, it was four in the morning and I was cold. My feet stuck out from below and my shoulders and arms were uncovered and it was then I realised that I had no covers save for the sheet because Z had pulled them all over to his side. That sudden jerk may have awakened me, when I suddenly woke up, when I knocked the cat over the side, when I sat up and said: *What the hell?*

Throwing my bare feet over the edge, I got up out of bed, untangled the cat, grabbed the edge of the covers from over Z and yanked my half over to me, said something to him about me having no covers and about his big butt jammed into the small of my back. He mumbled in defence: *What the hell?*

Regardless. It was time to get up. What the hell. May as well.

So I shuffled out of the bedroom, found the socks I had peeled off the night before, slipped them onto my cold feet, sat on the cold toilet seat to do this and to pee while the cat wound himself through my legs. It was dark and although I could feel his softness I could not see and I wondered if this fur body weaving through my legs as I sat on the toilet to put on my socks and pee was really what I thought it was, my cat.

We (the cat and me) padded off towards the kitchen and, turning on a light, I looked at the digital clock on the stove noting it was closer to 4:30 a.m. A reasonable time to get up.

Thus, my day began. I no sooner turned on the light when at my feet were my animals, my furry beasts demanding: *Feed me!* You can relate. At least this morning, for their sake, I'm not mad at the world for lack of sleep.

Is it happy hour yet? No, I did not succumb, although temptation was there, for under the sink, next to the wine, to the right of the bottle, I store kibble for the pets. I saw that bottle, heard her whisper to me in a slutty sing-song way: *I'm here! Yoo hoo; I'm here. Looky over here!*

I made it through another day. A good night's sleep helped to put a fix to that. No need to reach for the pinot noir today.

February 20

Good morning! Suddenly I'm reminded of an essay I wrote years ago, about a carpenter working at a house next door. I had gone to the front of my house to do yard work or something of that nature, when I looked through the chain link fence at the same time he looked my way. His job kept him at that house for days and I unabashedly prolonged my reasons for being in my front yard, fixated on him.

Mornin'!

It's the way he says it, the way he sings the word, 'Mornin'!' when he sees me first thing. I don't know if he's a carpenter, painter, drywall mudder or roofer, but when he greets me with his song, 'Mornin'!' well, my heart be still! Today, he called out "Mornin'!" from the top rung of a ladder. He was coming down from the second floor of the neighbour's house as I was emerging from behind our backyard fence, poo bucket in my right hand, latex glove over my left. Most mornings I try to remember to pick up my dog's poo before anyone steps on it, before the heat bakes it.

"Mornin'!" I called back to him over my shoulder. I could not see his face as mine looked into the rising sun. But I could sense he was smiling, could sense he was happy to see me. I

think he's been on that job for a month now, sometimes inside the house on the second story, sometimes fetching another tool or material from his work truck, sometimes just standing in the grassy lawn scratching his chin and thinking. Ah, how I love a man who can fix things! Ah, how I love a man who thinks. I'm guessing he could be twenty years my junior; certainly, he is tall. He wears his jeans low and his shirt loose. He has hair, light-coloured hair: sandy, straw, summer beach boy hair. I'll bet his eyes are blue, but I don't bet I'll ever get close enough to be sure. I'll bet his hands are strong, for that, I can be sure. I imagine us in a dance, his strong and calloused hand pressed against my back, just enough pull to draw me close. I imagine how he would tip a cowboy hat and sing 'Evenin'!' at the end of the day.

I drift.

It's a tad past 5:30. After four days at home, because his away-from-home work time on the road allows him comp days off, Z, by this time in the morning, has driven twenty-five minutes to the station to catch the 6:08. It's a bit dicey out there, blowing snow and I mean blowing. The fierce wind pushes snow against the kitchen patio door forming crests like wedges of whipped meringue.

Despite my opening greeting above, I'm not happy this morning; I'm stuck at *good* morning. I'm trying to fix that, sitting here in this semi-dark back-of-the-house room, door closed to keep out the cat, a pale green linen square draped over a fringed lampshade to cut down the twenty-five-watt bulb glare and a diffuser spraying an essential oil lavender mist into the air. Recently I introduced a pink Himalayan crystal salt lamp, shaped like a lava rock, to this lair with a fifteen-watt bulb tucked inside its base to make the pink salt glow softly. This lamp is said to emit ions – never can remember if they're negative or positive – clear the air, remove dust, pollen, mould, fungus and odours. Basically, it's supposed to extract cooties, supposed to help me breathe better, supposed to make me *feel* happy, promising the illusion of well-being and happy. Not a chance. It's going to take a lot more than a crystal salt lamp and lavender oil diffuser to clear my head this morning, make me happy. But I know and you may know what could: that voodoo elixir corked into the bottle hiding from me under the kitchen sink. If I think about the drink, I could make myself happy for the rest of this morning, knowing that by noon I just might reach for that calm from the bottle under the sink.

That's one thing I can say about Z. That guy wakes up happy every morning, no ions or mists required. He astounds me with his bright, cheery, positive outlook, like *Oh! It's five-thirty in the morning and overnight snow will surely make the drive to the train station treacherous but I don't mind. I'm so happy, so happy, so happy today, happy to get up and go to work today.* Egad! It's enough to make me want to swill that drink right now!

I wish I could just once, just once, experience the happy he feels every day, especially first thing, when he gets up to take on the day. I get up to take on a gorilla, no, I am the gorilla. And get this, he thanks me. He thanks me every day. *Honey, I'm nothing if not for you*, he says. *I'd be nothing if not for you.* Well, he gives me purpose to live, if not for my happiness, but for his.

I'm not sure at what point a person decides they've had a good life, or whether they made good choices, or whether their life circumstances were even fair. For myself, I'm finally learning to live with my *what is*. Unfortunately, there's no do-over key to push and so they realistically, pragmatically, go on. I can say, overall, despite lacking happy genes I wish I woke up with to take on the day, I've had a good enough life and given the do-over key to push I would not push it to do over again. Although, I have entertained thoughts, many times over, of having taken different forks in the road. Thankfully time is kind in that I've forgotten those other tines, dismissed the thoughts as foolish and ill-conceived.

I've been asked, often, what am I to do when Z retires, when he's not running out the door to catch the 6:08, when he's here with me, smack in the midst of my day to day, when he's under my feet day after day, when, unlike the cat, I just can't open the door and send him outside to hunt mice.

In fact, the cat did catch a mouse last evening, dropped it dead on the concrete slab, where I could plainly see through the glass the success in his hunt. I praised him to high heaven, *oh what a good cat you are, thank you for the present,* lifted him up and away from the prize and carried him inside, put on latex disposable gloves, a mouth mask and hazmat suit to collect and dispose of the poor thing. Poor thing.

Let me say this: on my husband's days off, when he's not running to catch the train, basically, he stays in bed, sometimes almost till noon, during which time I've already had most of my day, sometimes even a snort from the bottle I keep under the sink (that was before Lent) so that by the time he wakes up, plays with his doo-dad, I mean his laptop, has his coffee, oatmeal or eggs, all or any of which I serve to him with a linen napkin on a silver tray, by the time he watches his morning TV programs – he especially likes *This Old*

*Ho*use and *American Woodshop*, although frankly, he can barely turn a screw – by the time he's gone through what he calls his version of Deepak Chopra's *gentle wake*; when he's done lounging around, it's noon and I've had the better part of my day to do what I like to do or always do, manage the meals, pets and household chores, manage my husband while he's still in bed. Yes, I say to my friends, at least I know where he is.

Then, by the time he showers and shaves and trims his fingernails and comes out of his steamy bathroom, there's not much left of my day and what's left of his he either takes the dog for a walk or drives his truck into town to get gas and buy a burger or to visit a fly shop or some days, when he allows for enough time, he collects his gear: rod, waders, boots, vest with teeny tiny scissors, hooks, swivels and reader glasses tied with filament to the flap of a breast pocket, then sets out to troll the Pecos, sometimes the Rio Grande. Some mornings when I'm about my own business and he's still in bed, he gets out his special map and hunts up a new river to fish, where, if he's lucky he'll catch a brown or a rainbow with a fly he's tied and after he's ogled over the shine, glisten and beauty of this or that trout that he's lifted from the frigid fast-flowing river, he'll gently free it from the woolly bugger at the end of the line and set it back down into the stream where it wiggles away to live another day, to grow bigger, to be caught again by some other fisherman, or, quirky enough, to be caught again by Z. He seems to be able to identify previously caught fish. If we stay in these parts long enough, he'll one day come home to tell me he did indeed reel in the same fish. I can't tell you the countless times I've said: *Honey, bring home a fish. I want to eat fish.* But he never has, brought me a fish. Perhaps he doesn't want to please me after all, not like my cat, who beams when he brings me his catch of the day, a mouse, a bird, when he purrs up a symphony as he lays his love offering at my feet that day.

So when someone asks what will I do when my husband retires, I generally reply: *Nothing I'm not already doing; he has his life and I have mine and they're both good, both our lives and we don't complain either way.* Uh, check that, he doesn't complain ever.

I like to think about death. Maybe it's not that I *like* to, maybe I just do. Whoa there! I've never been suicidal. Much as I don't have the constitution for a hangover from drink, I have even less for doing myself in. Basically, I'm a wuss. And I think it takes courage to do one's self in. But that doesn't stop me from thinking about death, about what may or may not come after. I know very few people who do, think about death, not anyone who fesses up to it. Maybe no one. But I don't mind these thoughts of death and in fact, I feel comforted by them, because mostly, I think about all the brave fine and wonderful people who have already gone before me, wonderful people I have known from my living, the friend with the shotgun between his legs, a writing instructor with a disfigured face, other fine folk who have already gone before me whom I've never met, Mother Teresa, officially declared a saint; my murdered baby sister Mary, certainly a saint; folks long gone from over centuries of time, why, even Jesus himself, fine folk since time began, to present day. If they can go, so can I. I am comforted to think of an end to my own misery, however easily misinterpreted that could be.

I think about death, but not so much the transition; certainly I fear pain and loneliness and the possibility for violence and an unwelcome demise to come, but I do think about love and how much love I hold inside me that can only be released when, in the end, I finally cross over. 'Course, one has to wonder, why am I holding back? Why do I suppress this love, keep the genie in the bottle, waiting, wishing, for someone outside of myself to magically let love out? Why do I await the moment in death when I've had time enough in life to set my love free? Is this stifled love, the ache, the void, I try to soothe and fill with the drink?

February 21

Something novel. When Z vacated the bed to use the bathroom, I rolled over to his side to exit. I wanted to see if getting up on the other *right* side of the bed would fix my head, make me happy like him.

Here it is already, 5:30 a.m., he's gone out the door to catch the 6:08; the pets are fed, a load of whites whirl in the washer in the hall and I'm seated at my desk. Door closed to the cat but somehow the dog sneaked in and settled under the desk at my feet on a green cushy pillow pad. I won't concern myself for the dog walking across the keyboard. For now, she'll have to stay at my feet until I leave the room for coffee. And when I return, it's all beasts out! I'm beasty enough all by myself, with no help from my fur friends, no help from a drink, which, by the way I can say I managed another day.

But temptation threw herself on me like kerosene on flames. By 11 a.m. yesterday I was ready for that drink. In fact, in a way I cheated, pulled the bottle out from under the sink, popped the cork and inhaled. Fully. As vapours filled my flared nostrils, I inhaled more deeply, all the way down the hose to the chest where I stood there at the sink and breathed. It was enough. Now what am I guilty of? Vaping? Huffing? I learned about huffing when I worked on the rez.

Rohr writes about the challenges for seeking *full fun*. How one can get hooked on a high and then finds themselves locked in an eternal hunt for the next high. Although, to be fair to myself, it's not a high I seek from the drink. No, for me, it's the good company I find in the bottle, the congeniality of the genie herself, me myself. I am my own best company. I delight in finding the companionship of self when I drink. Otherwise, I'm basically lonely, not alone, because I'm quite accustomed to being alone and engage in those kinds of activities that lend themselves to going it alone, like reading a book or cleaning a toilet.

Something I need to be watchful for, however, is how that snort, or two, or three – let's just measure these snorts in ounces, not glasses – is how that snort influences me to seek *full fun*. Reminds me of when I was young – egad! I'm reminiscing about youth! Continuing…reminds me of when I was young and sought full fun in full sun, beaches bikinis and boys!

Yes, that's where I must be careful, in guarding myself against seeking full fun. Here's where I the author to this diary can get really revelatory about myself, because, for me, full fun can be turning not to the drink but, hang on, Popcorn! Or Ice Cream! Or Potato Chips! And yes! Even Extra Crunchy Peanut Butter and Strawberry Jam (Smucker's no less) on toast! Dangerous highs, carbs and sugar, dangerous to my other highs: cholesterol, blood pressure, glycaemic index. Dangerous me! And, I confess, I have a total disregard for portion size. Super-size me! Not to worry, I weigh in at one-twenty-three. However, problematic food and the drink are not the full fun I had in mind to be having; they're killing me softly, slowly, will win in the end.

February 22

Such a luxury, that sleep; like gold, like a sparkly diamond tiara that twinkles signals of royalty from the top of my head to under my feet; like a plush velvet robe about my shoulders I can wear the rest of the day. The rest of the day.

Such a rare commodity that when I do get sleep, when sleep does happen, I wonder with freshness what this new day will bring, because it is new and I didn't have to get up on the other side of the bed.

Here it is, six days left in the month. When I actually sleep, feel the benefits from a night-before sleep, I often awake to the idea of fun; I awake to the question: What can I do for fun today? Unfortunately, unlike my many other prolific lists, ideas for fun I can scribble on the pad of my pinkie.

I woke up this morning thinking about the myriad ways we kill ourselves. Not a very cheerful thought especially after I've expounded on feeling so good after a night's sleep, but the rest must have cleared the slate of my mind enough to think across the board. Heh, heh, heh.

There's a television series on the Justice channel about a medical examiner, a woman who goes by the name Dr. G. In the process of performing autopsies to determine the real cause of a mysterious death, her findings lead her to determine that death can result from a behaviour or practise that killed the victim softly, slowly over time. Death sneaks up through chronic overuse or ignorance or even innocence, by way of sheer disregard for consequences due to behaviour, like long-term consequences from taking too many pharmaceuticals, eating too much junk food and drinking too much wine. I know I'm killing myself – yet, why do I press my luck? With never enough sleep and with too much wine, carbs and sugar over time, I have to be killing myself. Better at my own hand, I reason, better at my own hand.

I think I may have written about a woman who lives nearby, near enough that when she sees me walking the dog, she comes out of her front door to join us. At first, she could hardly go the distance with us, me and my dog, so accustomed we are to go the distance, but she's catching up. On our walks together, we catch up with each other.

This woman – she's older by three years, divorced, no kids or grandkids, I'm coming to find out about her – lives in a house big enough for four but it's just herself and her aging cat – she recently won a local election to be a state delegate for the Democratic Party and then, suddenly stepped down. I couldn't believe it when she told me she quit! Just two days ago she won! This is something she wanted, dreamed about, schemed for, worked hard to attain, even shook up the neighbourhood when she solicited their votes using the Neighbourhood Watch contact list. The Republicans receiving the emails murmured: *She has her nerve!*

Want to know why she stepped down? Because her doctor told her so. *Missy,* he said, *you've been out of the hospital only three months. I don't want to have to put you back there again.*

It's too much! You've got to get well. Hotels and restaurants and convention halls are filled with ways to make you sick. No. You can't be a delegate because I don't want you sick.

She wanted this pretty badly, this win, this reason to live. And now, in mere minutes over the phone, her doctor snuffed out that slow burn of a flame that had put fire in her belly and gave her reason to live. 'Course, if she had snuffed out that cigarette fifty years ago none of this COPD business would've happened. Regardless, that doctor – what would he know of her real needs, what would he know about what's necessary for her to do in order to live? I would have told her to follow her bliss, stay in the game, all the way to her grave.

I don't know what's going on with me right now, but I need to quit writing because I'm getting all balled up in my own thoughts for her and her loss and maybe I've got it all wrong, maybe she did do the right thing, to follow her doctor's advice, but again, it's me I'm thinking about, my stubbornness for never following a doctor's advice.

I've got to stop writing now, unclench these tight jaws, spring myself free, let go of what someone else did that if I'm not careful, will hasten my own steps to the grave, which, what am I talking about? I'm the one ready to go.

It's hours later and I've come to realise that despite feeling awake earlier, ready to take on the day, to find some full fun, instead, all that energy I felt earlier in the day crested and now that plush velvet robe lies crumpled around my ankles and all I want to do is sleep. Who am I trying to kid? The drink is the trick, my fix, my own private bliss.

February 23

It's not working, this not drinking. Neither is sleeping. Just after four, I lifted myself up from my side of the bed like a corpse summoned from the crypt. To lie there while the march, march, march of thoughts crept like zombies on the prowl won't do nothing except bring on dread for the day. I couldn't let them have their way with me so I got up, planted both feet on the floor and quietly exited the bed, from my side, from the room, gently closing the bedroom door.

It's a good thing for me I have beasts that demand to be fed as soon as I patter in my re-purposed ski socks to the kitchen. I turn on the night light above the coffee pot and push its green button to start the brew, swing open the door to the cabinet under the sink where on the right sit two canisters: red for the cat, blue for the dog. But I can hardly distinguish colour in that dim of light; I just know the order in which I keep things. I open the cabinet door to the right because behind the door to the left sits my pinot noir.

Don't worry, at four in the morning I have no desire for the drink. Although a snort might be what I need to ward off the dread, get some sleep, knock me out and carry me off like a bride of Frankenstein. I'm so tired already I don't know how I will be able to push myself forward through this new day, for which, at the moment, I have no longing for fun, full or otherwise.

As Z finished his breakfast cereal and gulped his coffee, while he laced up his shoes, I said: *Honey, can you take me with you? Help me break the monotony of my day?* Of course, there was no reply. No answer for silliness such as this. Too bad for me it wasn't officially Take Your Wife to Work Day, then maybe he would have considered. No, it was a peck on the cheek, have a nice day, talk and text later.

Nowadays we don't call, we text. Good thing pets can't text. Good thing I can still open my mouth and hear myself talk aloud to my dog or my cat, to hear my wee little voice, be glad I can still hear.

Only he never calls, I never call; he'll text me to let me know he's boarded the train; he'll text to let me know he's back on the train at day's end. Only he never calls. Do you suppose he's having an affair? That's what I should be doing, having an affair. Can you imagine me having an affair? Married people today don't have to have affairs when they can turn on the Internet to turn themselves on, make believe that someone out there loves them, someone out there cares.

I feel like crap. As soon as Z's out the door, I'll hit the couch. *Columbo* comes on at eight. I could lock the doors, pull the shades, settle in on the couch and hope for sleep to come.

But when the garage door went down, I started up in the kitchen, washed the breakfast bowl, coffee cup, spoons, Z's plate from dinner the night before. Decided to take apart the refrigerator, pull out the drawers and wipe down the shelves. Decided to strip the bed and wash the sheets. Decided to vacuum, a chore I most disdain, because, mine is a man tool, an eight-gallon shop vac I use to sweep these bumpy-edged tile floors. It's so unwieldy, that long black hose thick as a python I sometimes throw over my shoulder to get control; that extra-large black tank tall up to my knees, a robot of a machine with a mind of its own, often refusing to follow behind me as I tug it down the narrow hall. Wheels wedge in the grout and there I stand with the python wrapped around my neck and the robot refusing to budge because he really just wants to be left alone. He's lonely too and wants me to take him back to the garage where he can be alone. I must not be good company to even the shop vac with a mind of his own, who'd rather I leave him in his room alone. Maybe next time I'll ask him to dance.

Murder She Wrote comes on at eleven. Maybe I'll hit the couch and hope for rest. Try not to think of chores, yet I do. But it's not working. Can hardly rise from the couch, except during commercials, when I roll to the floor to get up to let the cat out or let the cat in or wash up a few dishes or fold a few towels or reach for the peanut butter jar and jam and piece of toast to take back to the couch. During one of those breaks I'll pad to the bedroom to make up the empty bed with the clean sheets because I want it to look like I did something for the day.

At one point I switched from television to radio, coming upon a program that caught my ear and interest. Lying there on the couch I listened; it was a program on loneliness. Heart disease, depression, cognitive decline, these are just three effects mentioned in recent findings on loneliness. The radio discussion came about because Britain announced the appointment of a Minister of Loneliness to study the growing epidemic of loneliness and isolation. They should hire me. I'm an expert on matters such as these. The talk show panellists represented areas of expertise such as psychology, chronic disease and emotional wellness. They should include me on that panel, as a case study, case in point. Because this was a locally hosted program with local commentators dying to chime in. I learned that the state I live in, where I live now, ranks fifth in the nation in social isolation, due to so many living alone. Lonely people are subject to premature mortality similar to smoking fifteen cigarettes a day. Why, I'm no better off than my neighbour with breathing problems related to her acquired disease COPD, she who sleeps alone hooked to a machine. Hooked. We just can't live without our hooks into someone or something.

So that's the day it was all through the day, quiet, another without the drink. Who wants to have it that way? At least it's Lent and I can declare the sacrifice worthy because it's Lent. If anyone asks what I gave up for Lent I can say: my voice. I gave up the drink and my voice.

Not a word to no one all day. My neighbour texted me she would not be joining me on my dog walk because it was cold, because she was depressed (she did not say, but I could tell). I speak for her because she must be depressed, because I'm depressed for her, to have given up her seat as a state delegate for the Democratic Party, a lifelong dream of hers, to follow in her father's footsteps towards an active senior retirement as a fighter for the cause. She adored her father; he likewise her. I try not to muse about what it would have been like to have had an adoring father, one who doted on me with smiles and nods of approval, a gentle kiss on the forehead good night. Instead I got a drunk of a dad who'd sooner curse me, bust me in the chops.

Later in the evening, when Z came in through the door, when the dog rushed to greet him, his cheery, *Hi Honey I'm home*, seemed meant more for her than for me.

While I set his food on the table, he cracked a beer and sat down to eat with the newspaper to talk to him because having gone all day without a voice, I could hardly find one to ask: *How was your day?* To say: *I miss you.* To say: *I'm lonely, here at this house, alone all day.* A pitifully quiet, lonely day.

Friends, my friends: a cat, a dog, boob tube and yarn. No friends, no special things to do, yet plenty of things to do: drag the shop vac from room to room, dust the shelves, wipe the walls, take out the trash; plenty of chores and company to keep: a cat, a dog, boob tube and yarn; dishes to wash, towels to fold, toilets to swab, knitting needles and yarn and patterns too complicated I can only look at the pictures and wish. These, these, are my friends. But where are my talking friends? I should have been born before the invention of the telephone, before neighbours talked over fences; instead I live in the silent era: Internet, emails and texts.

February 24

And yet it's the solitude I crave. It's the being alone, in my own head, with my own bleak thoughts, in my own thin skin, alone with me and a shop vac and the dog and the cat, the pinot noir under the sink, in this tiny house, out on this sprawling desert sprouting with cholla that stick up from the snow-frozen ground like sparse kinked whiskers on an old woman's chin. It's the habit I am in and the route I have followed for too long to change now. Too long for even desire to awaken me now.

Of course, I could call; I could call you, my friend. There's nothing wrong with my hands that I cannot pick up the phone, plug in your number and call. But that would break the silence, throw a monkey wrench into the rhythm of my day, the bumpety-bump-bump rhythm it is, the sequence of things that seem right, day to day, day after day, the order of things I dare not disturb. It is what it is.

Then there's the *what if*, as distinguished from the *what is*. For so long I've learned to live without the question of *what if*, what if I changed course now? But how? Better not to ask, *what if*; better to accept *what is*. I do not dare change course now.

I don't know why I bother to babble. I've kept dozens of diaries over the years, most of which I've tossed, these dry and stale bread crumbs of my life. Better for me to sweep up my crumbs than leave for someone else. Better that the birds and coyotes and rabbits and gophers feed on my crumbs than leave for someone else. Better that I empty boxes, drawers, cupboards and shelves. I've always liked empty shelves – at times they held promise for things yet to come – save for the one under the sink, which holds all promise for what is now.

That radio program defined the difference between loneliness and isolation. As I understood it, loneliness is the perception of feeling disconnected. Making myself journal every day for one month at least gives me the perception of feeling connected, if only to me and an imaginary you. At least by journaling I can account for the dates on the calendar and at least I can find relief from humdrum with the drink; it's the writing and the bottle that bring relief; relief in tell-all confessions; solace in the sip-sip of the drink.

Yesterday I hit a wall. Must've happened sometime around noon, when I was oiling and waxing my cutting boards, when I couldn't stand it any longer and took to oiling the kitchen cabinets – the ones I did not finish when I started that project, what, maybe three weeks ago? – then I took to oiling the wood door in the living room and the wood French doors to the patio and then I went on to oil the bureau next to the coat closet and then the wood framed mirror under the entry light and then the hutch in the centre of the living room on which sits the TV and then before I could go on to find anything else to oil, I found the bottle of pinot noir under the sink.

Off came the gloves, the latex ones, off and onto the kitchen table – it's Formica not wood – followed by the oily rag and up came the bottle from under the sink and pop went the cork and out flowed the wine, but mind you, it was only a three-ounce pour, a juice glass sitting on the counter from breakfast, a little glass I took from a room at a motel. I never really intended to steal, but after six weeks in that transient cell I figured by then those glasses were as much mine as the next guy's. I think it's a well-worn theory on possession, that nine-tenths-of-the-law thing. We were staying at this roadside motel waiting for Z to be called up for his next assignment. Somehow two of those motel room juice glasses ended up in my possession and I've fancied them as perfect wine glasses for just that little sip-sip when needed.

Well, one three-ounce pour led to another and by early afternoon I had knit yet another hat and I had polished all the wood in the house and polished off half the bottle of pinot noir. Maybe a smidge more than half. For some reason I felt compelled to take on the stove, even though it was probably clean enough; I felt compelled to keep cleaning, proceeded to disassemble the entire stove top, removing the grates and burner caps, the overall lid that hides the tubing that brings fuel to the burners and when electrically clicked with the turn of the fat white knobs – the real reason I fell in love with that stove, because I loved the fat white knobs with a dot of red to indicate the on position – that when turned, bring a wreath of flames around the burners on which to set the pot to boil.

'Round about then, when I was pushing the vinegar-wiped knobs back on, my phone rang. And I had sense enough to take the call. Alas, a recorded reminder from the pharmacy telling me my eye drop prescription was ready; alas, not even a live voice to talk to.

Half. I stopped at half the bottle. In fact, I left half a juice glass undrunk on the counter. Did I lose my taste? My desire for the drink? Was I overcome with grrr for having broken my stretch of days without the drink?

No. No grrr. No guilt. None when I lunged for the bottle under the sink, none while I sip sipped, no grrr this day after, none while I spill my guts on this page. In fact, because I could not throw it away, that undrunken half glass sits on the counter still, a gnat floating atop. I'll drain the dregs sometime this morning, can't let it go to waste, when I'm doing the dishes would be a good time, so I can wash the glass and put it up into the cupboard. I don't know why I haven't thought to set the glass right next to the bottle under the sink where the glass and the bottle could set, well, like a set, at the ready for the next emergency pour.

I'll pluck the floating gnat out now before I forget, although the little guy is hard to miss. Can't tell if he's face up or down, but his wings float outstretched, almost as if he tried to backstroke to the edge but drowned instead. Not a bad way to go, little gnat, in a vat of pinot noir.

I'm wondering if maybe I could be sick in the head, like from dementia caused by breathing cat litter dust. I've sifted through cat litter every day for twenty-odd years, from different cats, three in fact, sifting through their litter to get every nugget of poop and cluster of pee because that's who I am, a natty litter manager. Maybe I've inhaled enough of that dust to damage my brain. I could donate my body to science and they could analyse it for litter dust damage to the brain. Studies conclude that she suffered dementia likely brought on by breathing cat litter dust, one percent of the ninety-nine percent dust-free cat litter dust.

It's cold outside. It's awfully cold. I don't have to go outside to know it's cold. And despite those few earlier days disguised as spring, overall, it's looking to be a long cold lonely winter this one. Sometimes I don't think my winters will ever end.

February 25

Mirror, mirror, on the wall. Who is my mother after all? I see her in me.

I don't stop very often to look at myself in the mirror these days, don't like what I see, the old woman looking back at me.

I keep a framed photograph of my mother on a bookshelf in this tiny room where I write, where the cat walks across the keyboard, where the dog seeks refuge under the desk when a clap of thunder startles us all. It's the same framed photograph I had set inside the white satin folds of her casket, leaned against her left hip, atop a lap quilt – one of her own crafting. I wonder what became of that quilt, if it went with her to her grave. Or did the brother who had driven a moving van up to her house during her church funeral take that, too?

The photograph of my mother was taken before her marriage to Frank, when she was a social debutante, a champion swimmer, a young woman already considered old by the time she married for good at twenty-five. Frank was not her first husband. She had married a man on his hospital deathbed, an Arthur, as he lay dying from a burst appendix.

This is my mother as I like to remember her in that photograph: a dark-haired, blue-eyed beauty meant for a kinder and gentler life than for beatings and babies.

Mirror, mirror, on the wall. Who is my mother after all?

Looking at her in the mirror looking back at me, I recalled a memory from a visit to her in Ohio, a morning when she and I sat at her round kitchen maple table covered with a red-checkered, flannel-backed vinyl cloth. For special occasions, she brought out a lace overlay. This wasn't one of those occasions.

Sitting together, sipping our coffee, she broke the silence with a confession, to a time before I was born. Realising she was pregnant again, she tried to abort me, me, her baby number four. *I tried to get rid of you*, she said matter-of-factly. *I didn't want another child. I'd had enough of your father and enough of you kids.*

She survived the attempted abortion and suicide and went on to carry me full term, not knowing whether I would be deformed in any way, crippled or brain damaged (so that's where it all began).

When I was little, before I learned to swim, I would never venture further out into the river unless I could touch bottom. When the water reached over my head, standing on my tippy toes, I would bend my knees, bounce up and down, eyes open, mouth closed, arms bent at the elbows and hands afloat. I was afraid of losing ground, losing control for my own safety, as I don't believe and I'm quite sure I'm correct on this, that had I drifted or slipped on mossy slime, lost my footing where I could not step to safety, I would drown. Never did I trust anyone to be there for me.

Our family was not well off, but we made do. The century-old dilapidated leaky-roofed, stained and faded brown-shingle two-storey drafty farmhouse sat on a double city lot on which we grew vegetables, raised and killed chickens and rabbits, played in a backyard sandbox we shared with alley cats. I wore my brother's outgrown faux leather black shoes stuffed with rags in the toes and my sisters' hand-me-down school uniforms. My mother darned our socks and resized pants and skirts to fit the next younger kid coming up.

Inside our house was a war zone. A hot spot of land mines, pin-pulled grenades, bombs exploding, invasions, bodies bruised, bloodied, spirits broken. Dresses torn; newly opened Christmas gifts fed to the furnace; bowls of spaghetti in homemade tomato sauce thrown against kitchen walls.

Recently, in conversation with another woman my age with whom I had hoped to forge a friendship, I let slip that my father killed my baby sister. At five, I had already developed a keen sense of what war was on the home front, whistles and sirens that even today, when a signal sounds, any and all hours of the day or night, whether tires screeching, a door slamming, or alone in the house when the teakettle blows, I want to run to take cover. For me, when it comes to fight or flight, it's run! Back then, when Frank knocked my mother down the steep, narrow, open backed, wooden cellar steps with splintered edges, seventeen of them, when the enemy went on the attack, recall for that particular ambush remains seared into my memory like a cattle rancher's brand.

I was there in the dining room, standing behind the drunk who did it, the brute who pushed open the door to the cellar and having grabbed my mother by the scruff of her housecoat – it was late at night, always late at night, in the late hours or the very early hours before light, before time to get up for school, children sleepless and scared, but ordered to stand at attention like little soldiers, having been dragged from their beds in their ill-fitting jammies and bare feet – the hours were always the darkest and coldest when Dr. Jekyll morphed into his Mr. Hyde, when Frank grabbed my mother, full term with their seventh child, by the scruff of her neck and shoved her backwards down the steps, like he often kicked the helpless dog, as he so often brutally did, down those steep dark creaky cellar steps. Forget turning on a light; he could never find the switch.

My mother lay there until morning – or was it already morning? – when one of us kids called our grandmother who rushed her daughter to the hospital to deliver a stillborn baby girl.

I remember as a helpful five-year old, that my mother tenderly included me in making a layette for the coming baby. I learned how to use a small hammer to pound metal snaps on flannel flaps, how to hem bottoms with a needle and thread, how to weave narrow bands of soft ribbon to gather and close openings around the neck. I remember that with the baby dead, my mother in the hospital, Frank collected the clothes and fed them through the iron door to that massive coal furnace where so much of my childhood burned up. Throughout the eighteen years I lived in that hell house, during those Catholic candle-lighting, scripture-reading, feast-fasting get down on your knees and beg for mercy hell-raising, praise Jesus years, I learned that possessions, no matter how precious, had no lasting value, or that anything could be valued at all, including children, because they were easily fed as fuel to that fire, anything Frank could feed to the fire to appease his madness. Those years in that war zone taught me not to love, not to cherish or treasure, because surely it would be taken from me, I would lose it, leave it behind, or destroy it myself.

The above story of baby Mary's death, the revelation, the confession I made to this woman my age whom I thought was someone I could befriend and trust backfired. Instead of a word of sympathy, empathy, whatever I had hoped to hear, she stared at me in disbelief at what I let slip. I have seen her once these few weeks since and our exchange was a brief and casual acknowledgement of the cold windy winter we are currently in.

It was HH, my younger sister by twenty-two months who found the letter. How she came across it is indicative of how my sister liked to rummage through our mother's house, especially her dresser drawers. This gal had a knack for sniffing out something that wasn't her privy.

The letter my sister purloined from my mother's dresser drawer changed hands from her to me when she decided she no longer wanted to be the one who had it. I have it. I came across it this last move, yellowed and splitting at the folds, tucked inside a plastic document sleeve, where it now sits in a basket where I keep such things, a kind of black hole for such things that have no other place.

I haven't read my mother's letter, written on the back of a church bulletin dated September 22, 1954, since maybe when my sister gave it to me and I just knew I had to hide it away. I do wonder whether my mother ever discovered that this piece of her private life was lifted from her dresser drawer. I seem to recall that when my sister gave it to me, nothing between us was ever said.

The other day, while reading Rohr, a point he was making stuck in my head. The gist of it went: *Some people decide not to hide from the dark side of things, but in fact draw close to the pain of the world and allow the pain to radically change their perspective. They agree to embrace the imperfection and even the injustices of the world, allowing these situations to change them from the inside out, which is the only way things are changed anyway.*

While writing this diary, without being conscious of the above, at this juncture in these final days of February, it's occurred to me to exhume that letter, that piece of history and read it again, mostly to examine who I am, whether changed from my past or whether more of the same, unchanged from the inside out. I've been writing in these pages about an aging isolated lonely woman still trying to discover herself, wondering if she's experienced a radical perspective as relates to her buried past, she lived a lifetime trying to avoid, to run from. Run. Run for it, girl, run. Or is it Run. Run from it, old woman, run.

Below, I've copied the letter of which I speak, written before the killing of Mary.

Dear Father,

I am writing this in hopes you can think of a way to save six children.

Since the day we married Oct. 4, 1941 my husband has been beating me. He says his children are not his. He worked in bars up to about three years ago. He never came in until daylight and he would beat me for having boyfriends. Now that he quits work in the shop at 3:30 pm, he never comes home for supper and if he does, he dresses up and goes out. He never comes home until he is so drunk, he's breaking furniture with his hands and saying to the children he's breaking up me. After I prepare what he asks for, he throws it at me. He'll drink beer and pour the cold stuff on my head and laugh. He slaps me down and kicks and spits on me. All the time he's slapping and pulling my hair he's trying to make me admit I'm having boyfriends. When he gets tired, he opens the door and throws me out. I'd go for good but I can't leave the children.

Yesterday he came home and demanded something to eat. I took the food into the living room and after he was through with each plate, he brought the remains into the kitchen and threw it at me and broke dishes and kept telling me how rotten I am. He keeps accusing me over everything. He kept slapping me and kicking me in the stomach and then he filled the bathtub with cold water and shoved me in. He tries to choke me and drown me and keeps trying to make me take poison or pills. Every day he brags about his women and demands that I admit I am doing wrong.

There must be a way to cure his mind for the children's sake. He says the church is no good, but I only have the church to turn to. Nobody is good but his women and drinking and gambling.

Father, what can I do? Can you help me and my kids?

February 26

My mother had asked her church for help and got none. How do I know this? Because after so many all-night drunks, the mornings after, we often asked her why she stayed. We begged our mother to leave our father. *Please, Mum, please, can't we get away?* She said she stayed because she loved him, because she loved us, because she loved her church. She believed in her church teachings. She trusted her priests. My mother's faith was rigid as rebar. The police were no help either. For all the times the neighbours called the cops, for all the warnings they gave Frank to sober up, they left our house and our safety all the worse for their visits. Frank would only drink and beat more.

Once, it only took once, when men in suits – two men in white shirts and ties, not missionaries but recovering alcoholics – when on a Saturday afternoon, I may have been eleven or twelve, they showed up at our front door. Frank threw their *Big Book* over their heads and a punch. Had it landed, he may have landed in jail, which never happened; he never ever went to jail.

I've suffered all my life from fear of abandonment, which seems at odds with how it really was, in the irony that I was never abandoned at all. I'm more the runaway than the one left behind. Indeed, we all ran away one time or another, even my mother, and the door was always locked when we returned.

From that radio program I wrote about a few days ago, one panellist mentioned how low self-esteem, how loneliness, can creep into our psyches like spreading black ink on a paper napkin; how the slow creep of loneliness leads the victim through a twilight zone where they lose perspective of self and surroundings. The lonely pull in like turtles to further protect themselves from what's out there.

For me, loneliness has always been my turtle shell inside which I take refuge and if for a moment loneliness leaves, I go back to where I last left her and crawl under her protective shield again.

Loneliness, the program went on, the condition of loneliness, the disease of loneliness, is worse than obesity. Today, February 26, would have been my oldest sister's birthday, the one who died twenty-two years ago at age 54 from loneliness out on the farm and consequences of obesity. I understand that loneliness can be linked to overeating and over-drinking. Most of my surviving siblings are fat. In fact, all but me. If we're not suffering from the consequences of too much food, we are suffering from too much drink. For the record, besides the sister felled by obesity and the baby felled by a kick down the cellar stairs, the drink has put the brother who loaded up and trucked away my mother's household furnishings while three of us were at her funeral, is currently serving time for assault. Brother JJ, plagued with diabetes, has also been charged with assault but survived sentencing; a sister who did not come to the funeral is lost somewhere in the la-la land of Las Vegas and HH, the purloiner of the letter, struggles with various physical and emotional trauma, two of which have left her hearing and speech impaired.

I'm the middle child, maybe in this I am lucky, to be able to look in either direction at what the drink can do to a family. Sometimes I refer to myself as a DP, a displaced person, like one of those immigrants from the old country who, sponsored by the church, were housed by my devout Catholic grandmother until they could get back on their feet, get a job, get established as Americans. It was always curious to visit my grandmother and learn that yet another gibberish-speaking stranger occupied one of the small bedrooms at the top of her dark mahogany stairs, cordoned off less one of us try to creep up to see.

These were lonely men, these drifters. I could say I'm a lonely drifter like them. Sometimes I think I shall die from my loneliness, a drifter finally spent from unrealised dreams, abandoned friendships, reckless marriages, spent on moving from here to there to anywhere. The radio program said I have a twenty-six percent chance of dying prematurely due to complications of loneliness, as my overeater sister did, out on that lonely prairie farm. In other words, I could eat myself to death, disease myself to death, drink myself to death, with the ever-so-slow drip-drip, sip-sip of my pinot noir.

While I drivel, my husband sleeps. He leaves today for a week-long assignment to various dots on a route that marks his pre-season training territory. He's somewhat of a drifter too, due to circumstances from his own childhood. A big difference between our dysfunctions, husband's and mine, is that he guards his misery like a jailor would his keys while I put mine out and take it down like laundry on a line. Up and down, up and down. The emotional roller coaster ride I can't get off.

Since moving to this desert, when Z takes to the road or skies for his work, I resort to being one of those displaced persons taking a room in my grandmother's house. While I'm saddened to see Z go, I quite naturally and comfortably take to my loneliness and to my room.

This morning, I'll wake him with a cup of coffee and a kiss, grateful to have him, because when he leaves, I'll slip into my turtle shell and call it good. I've pretty much quit trying to form healthy friendship bonds, trying to stay in a house or a town for good. Maybe I'm like my mother in one way, that I'm in this marriage for keeps. Sometimes I wonder if my husband really knows me and I often feel lucky he stays, but on the flip side, he's just as lucky I do the same.

Maybe the newly appointed UK Minister of Loneliness will begin the dialogue, begin to zero in on what we don't want to talk about. Maybe healthy families already do, well, that's not right, things like murder in the womb don't happen to them. Flawed families like my own breed bullies and rebels and mean-spirited patterns of behaviour for which we have no reliable understanding for how they got there. Our houses and families incubate serial killers, school teen shooters. Legislators talk about mental health, blame mass shootings on inadequate mental health monitoring, blame the parents, teachers, preachers and guns. Heck, a gun may very well be a lonely boy's best friend. And who would deny him that?

We, the collective we with whole-body childhood trauma tattoos don't talk about loneliness because we're already branded, ostracised, stigmatised and embarrassed. When we get to an age where we're supposed to join society – forget about blending – it's too late. We simply take our place among the outcasts of lonely.

By the time my husband departs for his week away, I will have already prepared myself for his absence, for the wake he will leave behind, for the void that backfills his wake, for my dodge under the safety of my hardened turtle shell, for my slip into an oblivion mine: walk the dog, knit another hat, watch reruns of *Murder She Wrote*, tango with that octopus of a vacuum, oil furniture, broom cobwebs from ceiling corners, knowing, always knowing it's there; hearing, always hearing, but not always answering to, the beckon from the bottle under the sink.

February 27

4:30 am. Empty house. Quiet. No one shouting at me to get out of bed, yanking the covers back from my head, demanding I get up, get downstairs and line up, stand and shiver at attention. Straighten up! No one lining us up as the Master Sergeant calls out the drills. No Mr. Hyde grabbing me at the throat, tearing at my pyjamas till the buttons pop. We wait barefooted, straight silent shivering. Tears begin to stream down our cheeks and our knees begin to give out as he undoes the buckle, slips the thick leather belt back through the loops, pulls out the strap, doubles it over. Which of us will it be this night? I must somehow deserve.

Empty house. Quiet. Nothing can ever get better than this. Empty house. Quiet.

I'm not an alcoholic; I'm not a drunk. I've not surrendered my life to the drink, although it's the drink that may very well sustain me in my day to day. I may have messed up a next day following a night of one too many and I may be somewhat of a reach-for-the-bottle-under-the-sink seeker of relief, but it's never been about emptying that bottle and having another. I've never sat at a table in the dark with a hand clutching the drink, or with my head in my hands, or with my head on the table; never again over a toilet. I sip. The bottle is never empty.

The last time I got drunk, unintentionally, unwittingly, was the Wednesday before Thanksgiving, two years ago. That would have made it about three weeks after this move, before the Mayflower arrived at this house with a boatload I had to subsequently rid myself of, treasures, friends and companions nonetheless, thrown overboard for someone else to discover, to enjoy, because it was too much for this tiny island in the desert upon which I was cast, before I was even awake to the series of events that landed me where I write from this desk today and I can say, where I am more awake than I have been in a long time.

I knew right then and there – I can picture us in the car in that trail parking lot, the dog in the cargo of the Subaru, the heat of an early July afternoon frying me through the untinted windshield like an ant under a magnifying glass – I knew, once again, my world, as I knew it there and then, for which I could not have known the consequences thereof – I knew when Z answered his work phone, when I heard him agree to the offer proposed, my here and now, as it was then, was over. Baked in the cake, stick a toothpick in it and call it done.

We moved a thousand miles across three states, went up from a green 4500 feet to a brown 7000. At a highway Mexican restaurant, not yet adjusted to what altitude can do to alcohol consumption, the first margarita having slipped down like an oyster on a half shell, I ordered a second. Later that evening, I was hugging somebody else's toilet bowl, the one in the bathroom in this house I've since made mine, but at the time, it was another squatter's bowl. Hell, I wonder if I had even cleaned it by then. Whatever, I laid claim to that cold white porcelain bowl that night, hugged it like I would the child I'd never had, but I clung to it nevertheless.

That was my last drunk. A two-margarita drunk. Not since then. And since then, I've not had another margarita, because I'm cured; I bounced off the bottom of that murky river, when I went bottom's up with that second tequila drink.

Not that I've softened the blow with an occasional reach for a sip-sip of pinot noir instead. Wait, yes I have. None of that hard stuff for me. Not in my sorry skinny constitution. When I can reach under the sink for a sip-sip of pinot noir instead. An aromatic concoction of red and black grapes, fermented and aged in French oak, with a note (a high note, get it?) of spice. Ting! I can just hear the ping of the fingernail flicked against the delicate rim of the glass, an oak-barrel-aged concoction rich in texture with a lingering finish, complementary to any cuisine, a sip-sip with finesse.

Who needs cuisine when a glass of wine all by itself will suffice? What do they call it, nectar? Food for the gods? For me, it's food for the soul. No wonder I'm skinny. The drink is both bread and wine. Light but filling, fresh but friendly, subtle but pithy, primitive, provocative, pleasing, restful yet restoring. Blah, blah, blah. Leave it to the crystal-clutching Californians to dream up this fodder. As I once was, among the very best, the berry best, of starry-eyed, fantasy-filled, beach-loving, deep-sea diving, boogie board surfing, California Girl. And now I'm the best among the none of them. Or so a tantalising sip-sip of pinot noir, the great emancipator, convinces me to believe, that I am, basically, despite my own label as damaged goods, normal.

Is that why I reach for the drink? If not to forget then to attempt a semblance to normal – and how would I know what a semblance to normal is? Do I reach for the drink in an attempt to rewrite history, to make sense of the madness that it was, wrestle with the loneliness distilled, an attempt to mend the flaws? I cannot reorder my DNA, no matter the abstinence cure I try to take. Because Frank is my DNA. Beer worked for him; wine works for me. But unlike Frank, I'm not a drunk. And unlike my mother, the forever-idolised victim of the drunk, a woman who never drank, I see no reason to abstain. A healthy happy woman she may have been before she married Frank; a healthy happy woman she did not make after. Healthy happy children she did not raise. I imagine myself somewhere in between these two, father, mother. Maybe that's the reckoning value of genes, to find oneself, stitched into a seam.

It's Tuesday – knitting day in the living room at the depot. I haven't gone for three weeks and I don't miss it. I feel somewhat remiss for not going because I think I made an unconscious decision to commit to attending when I went that first day back when. It's like kissing on a first date; you wonder later what you just did, if what you did means a commit. I don't do well with commit. Exception: Z.

In the beginning, my reasons to join these lovely women were because I was so lonely at home I could hardly stand to live, because I couldn't weak-eyed drive myself anywhere too far from the safety of this house, my shell, because I wanted to make friends. I'm a few years into this move, into this house and far more at ease with being alone, inside my shell, without a friend. I go to knitting now and then and nobody asks where I've been. You see? I'm not missed! I'm invisible after all.

Really, in most cases where I have to go and be among others, I steel myself to be with them, to appear and present myself as one of them, normal, because it's hard, when one is more accustomed to being alone, in their own company, near their own toilet, with loneliness their bestest of friends. I'm more like my mother in this case; she died at home alone. Or maybe like my uncle's common-law wife; she died at home alone on her toilet.

February 28

At the end of yesterday's entry, I said something about dying on a toilet. She did, my common-law Aunt Mabel; she did die on the toilet. She was living alone in my deceased uncle's house (Frank's brother) and when she suddenly quit showing up at the Oarhouse Bar across the street, on the corner, authorities were called to make a welfare check. Upon entering my uncle's house, they found Mabel on the toilet, dead for days. She died like a chicken with its wings spread to take flight. They had to break her bones to gurney her out of the narrow-doored bathroom.

Last night, I slept surprisingly well. Maybe it helped to know that today would be the end. Maybe it helped that yesterday, I did not have a drink; never reached for that bottle under the sink.

I dreamed I bartered with a woman, her bathtub for my long broom-handled spatula. What on earth would I be doing with a utensil such as that? But we traded, I got the bathtub and she got the spatula.

When I married, I entered into a bargain with my husband, only now I can't remember what we bartered over. I've reconciled that he didn't turn out to be the man I thought I married, but he can also claim I'm not the woman he thought he married.

I've been a willing partner to him and thus a willing partner to his absences and these moves, to the evolution of things as they are between us, to the rollout of my *what is*, as it is, today. I understand my life on the run began long before him, when I set out to get away as far as I could from Frank, his house, his strap, his get-me-another-beer, his drunken nightmares of the drums of war in the jungles of New Guinea pounding in his head as he took to beating his wife and kids.

I've gotten over the dozens of moves we've made over the decades due to jobs, due to the search for something better, due to hope for things different. No wait! That's not true; I've never gotten over all his absences, all these moves, all this runnin', all this confusion as to where I belong, where to call home, for what purpose is any and all? Furthermore, I don't think this displaced person is done with her life on the road. Any day my husband may tell me we're moving again.

I think it may be time to go home. Better, I really want to go home. When my mother was alive, when she lived in her tiny house in the middle of a woods, she would get lonely, call me across the miles and beg me to come home. I never obliged, but now I'm thinking it may be time to go home. But not home to her and her house, unless I'm saying I'm ready for my forever home. I'm beginning to think that we only live to die, to discover our forever home.

To borrow from Lyle Lovett, *It's closing time*. Time to put this experiment to rest, time for me to climb back aboard that conveyor belt, take my place in the here and now, move on with my old reliable life, ride it out to the end.

It is still Lent; this short month of February this year does not coincide with the end of Lent, but this last day of the month ends my journey in this journal. I'm at the end. While I did not succeed in what I set out to accomplish, abstain from the drink for a whole short month, I have nevertheless come to an end. I'm at the end and it's over. I shall plod on these rest of my days, yes, with my pinot noir under a sink, an anywhere sink and maybe next month it will be a cab, zin, or sangiovese. I'll sip-sip myself to the end and let the hand I was dealt play out.